THE TRUTH CHAMBER

BY

ROBIN BRANDE

THE TRUTH CHAMBER
A Winnie Parsons Mystery
By Robin Brande

Published by Ryer Publishing
www.ryerpublishing.com
© 2026 Robin Brande
www.robinbrande.com
All rights reserved.
Cover art by gatamotion, Jiro, and Lera Feeva/Canva
Ebook ISBN: 978-1-952383-72-4
Paperback ISBN: 978-1-952383-73-1
Hardback ISBN: 978-1-952383-74-8

ALSO BY ROBIN BRANDE

<u>Winnie Parsons Mysteries</u>

A Mind for Mysteries (Collection)

The Genius Track

A Man of Appetites

A Drop of Sweat

The Long Gray Hook

The Slip of a Rib

The Cabin Ghost

The Secret Juror

The Truth Chamber

<u>Dove Season Universe</u>

Dove Season

Finder

Seeker

Believer

Maker

Explorer

<u>Young Adult</u>

Evolution, Me & Other Freaks of Nature

Fat Cat

Doggirl

Replay

Into the Parallel

Caught in the Parallel

Seize the Parallel

Beyond the Parallel

Book of Earth

Book of Water

<u>Romance</u>

Love Proof

Freefall

Heart of Ice

Fire and Ice

<u>Self-Help</u>

What If You're Doing It Right?

What If You're Doing It Right? For Teens

<u>Collections</u>

The Love of a Good Dog

Mountain Tough

The Miraculous Unknown

Life with the Afterlife

Heart of the Future

THE
TRUTH
CHAMBER

"Oh, good. You saved me."

The monthly bookkeeping was something that had to be done, but it didn't mean Winnie Parsons enjoyed it. It was like cleaning the bathrooms and dusting: must be done, glad to have done it—but not necessarily glad while she was doing it.

But just as she neared the end of reconciling the credit card statement with her bookkeeping program, Winnie felt that familiar tug at the base of her abdomen. Like a small rock dropping in her insides.

A second later, her cell phone rang.

And Winnie knew without looking at Caller ID who was calling.

Amanda Birkauer—Dr. Amanda Birkauer, PhDs in both Psychology and Neuroscience—had been

Winnie's best friend and colleague for many years. Winnie knew a kindred soul when she found one.

Twenty-five years ago, Dr. Birkauer had only recently joined the faculty of the University of Arizona Psychology Department when the annual Brain Day came up on the schedule.

A Saturday event when faculty and students could showcase their most fascinating research projects.

Winnie loved to see what everyone else was working on. She stopped showcasing her own work once she achieved tenure—for reasons those who knew her best understood—but she still loved to come poke around and observe. People were so clever. She loved seeing what everyone was up to. It always inspired her.

Dr. Birkauer had been newly hired as an associate professor after graduating from Purdue and then Oxford.

Winnie had a soft spot for anything British. In another lifetime she would have loved to attend Oxford herself.

In another lifetime, in fact, maybe she had. She didn't know either way, but she wouldn't put it past herself.

Winnie knew what Amanda Birkauer looked like, from her picture in the faculty bulletin that month. Winnie scanned the crowd at Brain Day, and quickly found her.

Dr. Birkauer was in her late twenties then, sporty-looking with long brown hair she wore in a high pony-tail threaded through a University of Arizona navy blue baseball cap. In fact, she was decked out in all U of A attire: navy blue running pants with *Wildcats* printed in red down the sides; a bright red UA Wildcats T-shirt; a navy blue windbreaker with UA Faculty printed on the front.

The only way she could have shown more school spirit was by waving a little U of A flag.

To this day, Amanda still typically dressed that same way: running pants, T-shirt, a zip-up windbreaker or hoodie if it was cold, all of them bearing the University of Arizona logo. She still threaded her long brown ponytail, now laced with strands of gray, through her U of A baseball cap. It was as if she had chosen her uniform on the first day of school, and there was no need ever to change it.

"Welcome," Winnie said, handing her a slice of carrot cake on a plate. "Tell me all about the accents."

Amanda accepted the cake and dug in with the white plastic fork. She took a bite before answering.

"Gorgeous."

"Cake or accents?"

"Both," Amanda said.

"Were you ever tempted to start speaking that way?"

"All the time," Amanda said, taking another bite of cake. "Couldn't pull it off."

"I probably couldn't, either," Winnie said. "But I'd want to do it so badly."

"That's why I can't go to Australia," Amanda said. "Not a chance on that one."

The two colleagues grinned at each other.

You'll do, Winnie almost said out loud.

I want to be your friend, also might have slipped out.

But Winnie slipped back into professionalism and formally introduced herself as a fellow professor in the department.

"What subject?"

"Consumer Psychology," Winnie said.

"Good one. I'd like to hear about that."

"You first," Winnie said. "I'm going to need you to come have lunch with me and tell me everything about Oxford."

"Will do," Amanda said. "Thanks for the cake." She gestured around the crowd with her plastic fork. "Anything you think I should know?"

Winnie laughed. "Oh, yes."

She could have sworn Amanda's eyes lit up with a mischievous sparkle.

The young professor checked her watch. "Oh, look," she said, even though it was only a little after nine A.M., "it's lunchtime already."

Amanda Birkauer was an onion to get to know. Lots of exterior razzle dazzle, lots of layers, all of them impressive enough, none of them revealed through any kind of bragging.

They would just come out, here and there.

"The year I spent in Spain…"

"When I did that diplomatic internship…"

"That round I did at the morgue…"

"How old are you?" Winnie asked at one point early in their friendship. "Because you have to be at least a hundred to have done all the things you've done."

"Multitasking," Amanda answered. "It's amazing what you can pile on."

It also helped that she only needed about five hours of sleep a night. Winnie was no good without at least seven. She was fifteen years older than Amanda, but it wasn't a matter of their ages. Amanda Birkauer was obviously born with extra gears.

And it wasn't just in her professional life. Amanda also had a separate athletic life she didn't advertise to the rest of her colleagues. But Winnie discovered it quickly enough.

As the two of them stole away from the Brain Day exhibitions and sought out the food tents set up on the grassy mall, Winnie caught a brief glimpse of this new professor's other life when it suddenly flashed across her mind.

"You're a runner?" Winnie hadn't meant to blurt it out, but sometimes her mouth did that.

"Um … kind of."

And a swimmer. And a rock climber. And a cyclist. And—yes, there she was, sparring at a gym—a boxer.

Winnie did a quick reassessment of the woman walking beside her.

"Triathlons," Winnie said. It was a statement, not a guess.

Amanda smiled. "You are very good at this. What's my middle name?"

Winnie was rarely tempted to show off—in fact, just the opposite. She usually kept her abilities as private as possible.

But something about Amanda's tone made Winnie want to answer. Like they had known each other all their lives, and this was a game they had always played.

"Gable Rae," Winnie answered, not knowing why those were the names, but certain that they were.

Amanda stopped in her tracks. She stared at Winnie with a look of delight.

"Oh my god," Amanda said. "Right out of the chute. This is how it works."

"How what works?" Winnie asked, feeling now like she had said too much. What had gotten into her? When had she become so reckless?

Amanda leaned in. "Do you know why I'm really here?"

Winnie shook her head.

"Come on," Amanda said. "I bet you do."

She gave Winnie an expectant smile. Encouraging her. Maybe challenging her.

Winnie saw the cards. One by one, Amanda holding them in front of herself, while a young female student sat across from her at a wooden desk in some small bookcase-lined room. Winnie could smell the books. Leather-bound and old. And there was a lingering tobacco pipe smell, like someone's grandfather might have just left the room.

Amanda drew the next card and looked at it.

Winnie studied Amanda. Like watching a close-up from a movie playing just for Winnie inside her mind.

Amanda Birkauer looked younger, but not by much. Maybe around twenty-five or twenty-six. She wore a white button-down shirt—an *Oxford*, Winnie realized —with a thin black tie at her throat. Over both she wore a thick gray wool V-neck sweater. She looked very dapper. A proper English scholar.

The girl sitting across the desk from her had dark curly hair and wore an oatmeal-colored wool sweater with a thick blue scarf that brought out the blue in her eyes. Right now she closed her eyes for a moment and concentrated.

When she opened them again she said, "Star," in a light and lilting British accent. Quite lovely.

"Correct," Amanda answered in her plain American accent. She set the card with a star on it face down on the rest of the deck. She drew another card and studied it.

"Wavy lines," the student said.

"Correct," Amanda said, and Winnie could see that it was.

The cards were part of an ESP deck. Extrasensory perception. Winnie knew all about them. They were called Zener cards after their creator, Karl Zener. They were the standard in parapsychology research to test someone's psychic and telepathic abilities.

Winnie had once—foolishly, she realized in the middle of it—volunteered to participate in a study one of her colleagues in the psychology department was conducting to see if the cards really worked.

Winnie didn't want to do it. She didn't need to do it. She had known since she was a little girl that her mind operated differently from other people's.

But ... something drew her. Curiosity, she assumed, since that was usually the reason she did anything outside her normal routine.

Winnie had been hiding her clairvoyant gifts for most of her life by then. She had no desire to expose them to anyone, let alone a fellow faculty member. People's responses could run anywhere from fascination to fear. Usually, fear. Winnie had a very safe, satisfying position at the university, and it made no sense to jeopardize it.

But the colleague running the experiment was a

friend, and by the time Friday came along that week, Bernadine was desperate. She had reserved lab space and camera equipment and advertised in all the places they usually did to attract volunteers among students and university staff and faculty and even people in the community—and no one had come forward. Not a single person.

"I can't fail that completely," Bernadine said. "I've been talking about it for weeks. Please, Winnie, let me get at least one set of data. This is embarrassing."

So Winnie decided, for the sake of friendship—and maybe at least twenty percent out of curiosity—to give up an hour or two of her Saturday morning to sit at a lab table and be filmed guessing every card wrong.

That was the challenge Winnie gave herself. She was going to be a hundred percent wrong. If she accidentally said the right thing, she lost a point on her own personal scoring sheet. She was going to prove that she didn't have a single ounce of psychic ability. Bernadine wouldn't be surprised about that. She would probably expect it.

Psychics were special. They were woo-woo and mystical. Winnie was a just a boring psychology professor. She lived alone in a townhouse a few miles from campus and usually rode her bike into work. No pets. No significant other. No exciting vices. She preferred to spend her Friday nights at home reading a good mystery novel or watching a movie rather than going out drinking with her fellow professors. She wasn't unfriendly—far from it. She had lots of friends in the department—but she liked her privacy and her quiet. Nothing wrong with that.

And Winnie had learned the hard lesson back in her twenties that no one really wanted to be with someone who might know as much about them as Winnie did. People felt very exposed. Vulnerable. Even though Winnie's insights into their lives and personalities and feelings could just as easily come from her understanding of psychology as her from clairvoyance.

But the few times she let herself slip and revealed information she had no logical way of knowing, she ended up paying for it with lost relationships. She prided herself on learning from her mistakes. It was a mark of maturity and wisdom.

It was also pure self-protection. Winnie wasn't stupid.

By the time her friend Bernadine begged her to come sit for the experiment, Winnie was thirty-four and very comfortable with her well-rounded life. She didn't want or need any more than what she had. And as for love, she had a brother and his children to give her all the family she needed.

But Winnie's path led her one way.

And on a Saturday morning in a lab in the basement of the Psychology department, someone else's path led to that exact same spot.

2

He was tall. That was the first thing Winnie noticed. She was five-foot three, average weight, plain, as far as she could tell, and never bothering to try too hard to up her appeal with makeup or any kind of hair style or fancier clothes than what she usually wore to teach: dress pants, button-down shirt, maybe a professional-looking jacket if she wanted to take it up a little. She wore her wavy light brown hair in a simple cut just above her shoulders. Wet it, comb it, good to go.

That Saturday, October 11, the weather was still warm. Tucson's temperatures wouldn't start feeling like winter until early December.

Normally on a Saturday at home Winnie would be cleaning and cooking for herself for the week. Maybe head out for groceries or some other errand, but generally just hang out at home in T-shirt and shorts or sweats.

She wasn't going to dress up for the lab work, but she wasn't going to show up looking like a slob, either. She chose a pair of jeans, a white cotton T-shirt, and a loose denim overshirt. Nothing special, nothing memorable.

When she saw him, she felt … what else could she call it but a recognition?

He was talking to Bernadine, this tall man with excellent posture wearing khaki slacks, new-looking sneakers, and a short-sleeved light blue button-down shirt tucked in and bordered by a belt.

Winnie saw him and took a small step back. She suddenly felt underdressed. It was so strange. She shook off the thought.

She didn't think of herself as self-conscious. Or vain. And yet for that moment she wished she wore her regular professor uniform to seem more impressive.

Ridiculous. Stop it.

Bernadine greeted her and resumed describing the experiment to the man. But he wasn't paying much attention. His warm brown eyes held Winnie's gaze. She cleared her throat and turned away. "I'll be back in a minute…"

She escaped into the hallway.

The lab room where they were meeting was smaller

than any of the classrooms. It held a row of four wooden tables with chairs on opposite sides. Psychology experiments usually involved a questioner and a subject, sitting across from each other.

Winnie had participated in experiments from both sides of the equation. None of this was new to her. Bernadine wasn't going to have to explain any of it to Winnie.

But right now, standing in the hallway outside the lab, Winnie felt incredibly nervous. She knew it wasn't because of the test. It had to be that man.

She blew out a breath. Told herself to calm down. Her heart wasn't exactly fluttering—that wasn't it—but it did feel like it was beating a few extra beats.

She almost turned around and biked home right then. This whole thing was ridiculous. She wasn't a teenager. She wasn't a girlish ingénue swooning at the sight of some new man.

That wasn't how Winnie's heart or mind operated. She was far too practical for that.

But that feeling of *recognition*. It was real. And Winnie realized that was the problem. This wasn't the reaction of a normal woman to a tall, handsome stranger.

She was reacting like a clairvoyant.

That was where she had to look.

Winnie closed her eyes. Calmed her heart. *Show me,* she asked her deeper mind.

What she saw made her eyes spring open.

She wasn't sure whether to laugh or run away.

But she was sure of something, and that was that her mind had shown her the truth. Winnie never doubted that. Her mind was her most reliable partner and friend. It never, ever lied to her or steered her wrong.

Winnie had made plenty of mistakes over the years, but that was from not following what her mind was trying to tell her.

So she had a choice right now: Stay or go? Accept or run away?

Her legs felt weak. Her palms were sweating. She felt light-headed. It was all so ridiculous.

Don't be a coward, she heard herself say inside her mind.

Winnie sighed. Things were about to change. Not just a few things—*everything*.

Winnie steeled herself. Straightened her own posture to match the man's who stood on the other side of the door.

Then she pulled the door open, let her green eyes lock onto his, and she made herself relax as she let the experiment begin.

Nine years later, on another beautiful Saturday morning in October, Winnie met Dr. Amanda Birkauer at the Brain Day exhibition.

As they sat at a white plastic table under the food tent, sharing a giant paper plate of nachos—at 9:15 in the morning, even though Winnie had already eaten oatmeal and fruit for breakfast—Amanda still wasn't saying why she joined the faculty at the University of Arizona. She was still waiting for Winnie to divine it herself.

And Winnie already had. But she wasn't ready to say it. Because the implications were uncomfortable. She wanted to enjoy this conversation with a new potential friend without adding any layers of conflict.

"I think you know," Amanda said, giving her a piercing look. "In fact, I'm sure of it."

Winnie shrugged and pulled out another cheese-smothered tortilla chip. She dipped it in her plastic cup of spicy, excellent salsa. The restaurant the food booth belonged to was one of Winnie's favorites. Their bean burritos were too big for a regular dinner plate. They had to be served on a platter. Winnie always told herself she'd eat just half and save the other half for later, but somehow she managed to clean her platter every time, and then didn't need any other meals for about the next two days. Perfection.

Amanda tipped back her baseball cap and leaned across the white plastic table. There were people sitting at a few of the tables nearby, eating *heuvos rancheros* or giant cinnamon buns or other breakfasty snacks, but none of them were paying attention to Winnie or Amanda. Why would they? A middle-aged woman who was clearly a professor and a younger woman who looked like she might work in the athletic department. Nothing interesting about that. Winnie knew their conversation was completely private.

But even though the risk of exposure was low, she still didn't want to say it. She knew she liked Amanda Birkauer—instinctively and immediately—but decades of habit had made Winnie keep her secret to herself. It was always safer that way.

Amanda Birkauer gave Winnie an encouraging smile. "Come on. I can tell you're not the kind of person who's going to make me beg."

"Really?" Winnie asked. "How can you tell?" She continued chewing her nachos and avoided Amanda's eyes.

But already Winnie could feel her defenses weakening. Even asking Amanda that question was a step in the wrong direction.

"Because I don't like people like that," Amanda said, "and I already like you. So." She leaned back again and pulled the brim of her cap snugger against her forehead. Like some kind of sign from a catcher to a pitcher: *Curve ball. Fast ball. This batter's gonna swing.*

Winnie sighed. She leaned away from the table now,

too, and risked looking into Amanda Birkauer's lively gaze.

Winnie muttered something.

"If you're cussing me out," Amanda said cheerfully, "I didn't quite hear that."

"Assistant Director of the Parapsychology Lab," Winnie said more clearly. She might have made it sound a little like cussing. "They're reviving it. I sort of knew something about it a few months ago. But I was hoping it wasn't true."

"Because…?" Amanda prompted.

"The last time was a disaster."

Which felt almost like a betrayal to say, since Winnie had met the love of her life there.

But there was no question things had gone quickly downhill after that. Her friend Bernadine eventually quit. It wasn't a happy memory—at least that part of it.

"We're going to do it right this time," Amanda Birkauer promised. "Wait and see."

Winnie gave a small shrug. It didn't have anything to do with her. She wished this new professor well, but considering their paths, this might be the last time Winnie shared a meal with her.

"What are your clairs?" Amanda asked.

Winnie could have pretended she didn't understand the question. But she did. It didn't mean she had to answer.

"Clairaudience," Amanda recited, counting them on

her fingers, "clairvoyance, clairsentience, clairgustance—"

The sound slipped out before Winnie could catch it. A light snort, the way a kid might snort at a fellow student who had just made a fool of himself in class.

Clairgustance was an inelegant name for a strange ability Winnie only rarely felt: being able to taste something without it being in her mouth. She once tasted a Butterfinger candy bar her brother Steven was furtively eating underneath a scraggly bush near a Circle K in their neighborhood. It was Winnie's first clue that something was wrong. Then she saw the rest of the mini-movie in her mind: Steven and his friends had all dared each other to shoplift something. This was Steven's version of the crime.

Winnie confronted her older brother about it the moment he walked through the door of their house.

"I saw you."

"No, you didn't."

"I could taste it. Butterfinger. You're busted."

Her family knew all about Winnie's abilities. It had been an adjustment at first—she couldn't imagine any family would automatically know what to do with a clairvoyant child—but by the time Steven stole the Butterfinger, he and Winnie's parents had already learned to take her abilities in stride. No one was going to kick her out or ostracize her just because she could taste chocolate and peanut butter she hadn't eaten.

It wasn't so easy explaining to the boyfriend Winnie dated for a few months in college why she knew he was lying about where he had been. She could taste the vodka on his tongue … an hour before he showed up at her apartment and claimed he had just woken from a nap. "Sorry I'm late. I overslept."

"Um … you didn't. You were at a bar with your old girlfriend." Winnie knew it was reckless of her to say it, but she felt too angry and justified to keep it inside. First the taste of vodka had invaded her mouth, then the whole scene played out in her mind. She could see the two of them drinking and pawing at each other. It was only a matter of time. The relationship was clearly over. But Winnie had no patience for any lies.

"What, you followed me?" the boyfriend demanded. "That's sick. You have a problem."

He left in a huff and that was that.

So yes, it was one of her clairs. Not one that brought her any pleasure. It wasn't as if she could taste the scrumptious-looking cinnamon roll that young woman was eating over at the next table.

"You know what I'm going to ask," Amanda said.

"And I respectfully decline."

Amanda surprised Winnie then by suddenly standing up and wiping her hands on the paper napkin that came with their nachos and tossing the napkin in a perfect arc that landed in the plastic garbage bin a fair distance away. All in one smooth, continuous move, as if she had practiced it over and over.

Winnie caught a flash of that, too: high school-aged Amanda Birkauer running the basketball court, fans in the stands cheering as she paused and lined up her shot and sent the ball upward in a perfect arc that landed in the center of the basket. It fell with a quiet swish. Nothing but net.

"State champions," Winnie said. "Two years in a row."

"You can't resist me," Amanda said with a smile. "It'll be fun. You'll see. I promise."

She was right, Winnie didn't want to resist her: not her friendship, not the fun, not any of it.

Even if it might turn into another disaster.

But somehow Winnie didn't think so.

And there was something else. Maybe it was because of the way Amanda spoke about Winnie's abilities as if none of them were a surprise, but Winnie felt in that moment, there in the food tent, the giant plate of nachos nearly polished off between them, that she could let down her guard around this person. That she could actually be honest with Amanda Birkauer.

That was a rare feeling. One Winnie didn't take lightly or dismiss.

In fact, something about Amanda Birkauer made telling the truth feel like the most relaxing thing in the world.

"It has to be anonymous," Winnie told her.

"Of course. No problem. We'll assign you a number. We'll never use your name."

It was how Dr. Winifred Parsons came to be Test Subject 2143.

"You already have over two thousand subjects?" Winnie asked when she heard the number. She was both shocked and impressed.

Amanda scoffed. "Never start at zero. You look like an amateur."

Winnie incorporated that into one of her own Consumer Psychology lessons the following week. Because Amanda was absolutely right. Perception was everything. Telling a customer that thousands of people had already bought this product confirmed them in the wisdom—and coolness—of their choice.

Was agreeing to be one of the parapsychology lab's test subjects wise? Was it cool?

It had certainly led to knowledge Winnie knew she couldn't have uncovered herself. Amanda Birkauer and her boss, Dr. Robert Kuhlman, took their time rebuilding what they rebranded as the mind lab, and before long they were able to attract a steady stream of volunteers eager to test their abilities. Volunteers not just from among the University of Arizona faculty and student population, but ultimately from around the world.

Birkauer and Kuhlman took psi abilities seriously.

They were clearly doing real science. They didn't apologize for believing that psychic abilities were real and that they could be measured and—more important, from Winnie's point of view—improved.

The idea that she could learn more and build her own skills was very, very attractive.

And the fact that she could do it in secret, as anonymous Test Subject 2143—that was the best part.

And now, on the phone with Winnie, saving her from having to finish her boring but necessary bookkeeping, Amanda Birkauer laid out some very tempting bait.

"The Brits are here," Amanda said. "And a few Russians. I've had two days with them already, and I think you'll love what we're doing tomorrow. It's their last day. Are you in?"

Winnie saw a flash of what Amanda had in mind. Little snippets of the experiments on her agenda.

Winnie laughed. "It looks crazy," she told Amanda, "but yes, I'm in."

"Not to make you competitive," Amanda said, no doubt knowing that was exactly what she was doing, "but some of these people are gonna to blow your mind. Can't wait to get you in a room with them."

When they hung up, Winnie stared at the bookkeeping program still open on her screen.

She had made a promise to herself three years ago when her whole life took an unwelcome turn that despite her sorrow and the pain, she would still keep her spirit alive.

And part of that, she realized, was the new motto she created for herself: NBB. Never Be Bored. Otherwise her wounded spirit had nothing to look forward to when she woke up every morning. Winnie still wanted to learn. She *needed* to learn. It had been the constant thread in her life.

She closed out the bookkeeping program. She could finish that tedious chore later.

Thanks to her friend Amanda Birkauer, Winnie was about to engage in another new project guaranteed to help her keep her promise to herself.

3

"Clover, sweet girl, come here." Winnie held out the yellow Labrador's favorite consolation treat, a veterinarian-approved digestible mock rawhide chew.

"You, too, Arthur. Come on."

The little King Cavalier Spaniel trotted on his short legs to come sit next to his little—though larger—sister on the light blue kitchen rug.

His original owner had given him the regal name of King Arthur, but now that he had lived with Winnie and Clover for a while, Winnie found his full name a bit of a mouthful. Arthur it was.

As much as she loved animals, Winnie had never had a pet of her own before Clover. Her mother wouldn't allow it when Winnie was growing up, and even though Winnie always meant to get herself a dog, she just never seemed to find the right time.

Clover, now seven years old, had been a surprise gift. Well, almost a surprise. Joe had done his best to keep the information out of his mind for a whole day, but Winnie saw the little puffy furball with the pearly-white teeth and bright red tongue a full minute before Joe brought her into the house.

What a delight the dog was then and every day since. What would Winnie do without her? And though Arthur had been a surprise addition to their little family of two a little over a month ago, now it felt as if he had always been the missing piece.

"I'm going to be gone for a few hours," Winnie explained to the dogs. Did they really understand her? Winnie still wasn't sure. But it didn't stop her from narrating their life together and always keeping Clover and now Arthur in the loop.

Their neighbor Dawn was out of town this week, otherwise Winnie would have left the dogs with her to spend the day mostly lounging around with Dawn's long-haired Dachshund, Sporty. But this was the best Winnie could do for the dogs on short notice. She was happy that at least they could keep each other company.

She had already taken both of them on their early morning walks. The days were getting lighter earlier now in mid-March, but the air was still nice and cold.

Winnie could bundle up in one of Joe's old flannel shirts and her purple fleece vest and enjoy Tucson's version of winter. Sunny, mild, crisp—exactly the way she loved it.

Now that Arthur was with them, Clover got two walks. The first was just a short stroll around a few blocks of Winnie's university neighborhood. Arthur was still recovering from a few health problems, so she wanted to be careful not to push him too hard.

Then while Arthur rested at home, Winnie and Clover took their second, longer walk on the nearby University of Arizona campus. There was frost on the grass that needed rolling in. There were students and professors to greet. If there happened to be one of the campus shuttles parked at the curb with its door open, waiting for passengers, Clover always climbed aboard. The drivers were used to her and lavished her with affection. If the Lab cast a side glance at their bagged lunches up near the bus driver's seat, she was too polite to actually steal it and run away. Although there were a few times Winnie wondered.

Then after doing the full circuit all the way to the end of campus and back, Winnie and Clover and now Arthur would usually spend the day together doing their lives side by side.

Winnie hardly traveled anymore. She had friends all over the country and some in Europe and Canada, but Winnie would rather host them all in Tucson to let them escape their harsh winters than leave her dogs with a sitter or at a kennel. Maybe Clover and Arthur wouldn't mind, but Winnie would. She loved the dogs and wanted to spend every day with them.

Maybe she was making up for a pet-less childhood. Or maybe spending every day with Clover in particular was a way of keeping Joe close by. Or maybe, Winnie accepted, she had just come to a point in her life where she liked her nest and liked her routines, and the dogs were part of that satisfaction.

And as far as she could tell, the dogs were just as satisfied with the whole situation as she was. They certainly seemed satisfied now stretched out on the kitchen rug together chewing their compensatory treats while Winnie locked the door behind her and headed off to campus.

She dressed for comfort in a loose pair of hiking pants and a soft white T-shirt with one of Joe's blue flannel shirts on top. Not that different of a look from the first day she met him during her friend Bernadine's parapsychology experiment.

Winnie still wore her wavy hair loose in a cut just above her shoulders. Her hair was white-blonde now and had been for many years. Sometimes she saw pictures of herself with darker hair and had no memory of ever seeing that look in the mirror.

She kept fit by walking and walking as long as the weather allowed it. She could usually keep it going from early October to mid-May. After that, she continued taking Clover on her campus walks before 6:00 AM, before the asphalt and sidewalks had heated up too much for Clover's paws, but Winnie shortened their route, brought Clover home for breakfast, then walked alone to the university rec center for half an hour of laps in their pool.

She always loved to hear about Amanda Birkauer's various marathons and triathlons and other endurance sporting events, but Winnie felt absolutely no pull toward doing that herself.

"I'm a Labrador," she once told Amanda when they were discussing their different tastes and personalities. "I was built for the long slog. Then I just want to relax somewhere soft and cozy."

"And what am I?" Amanda asked her, crunching down on a tortilla chip. They were sharing another plate of nachos at another Brain Day event several years after their first one. Nachos for breakfast had become their signature move.

Winnie considered her friend. "A whippet. No—a German Shorthaired Pointer."

Amanda chuckled. "That's specific."

"A friend of my brother's had one," Winnie said. "His name was Blue."

"The dog, not the friend," Amanda guessed.

"No, the friend's name was Rover." Winnie gave her a sarcastic look. "Anyway, he was a fabulous dog.

Totally soulful. You'd look into his eyes and there was definitely someone there."

"I love that," Amanda said.

"And he was great around the house," Winnie said. "Polite and low-key. Perfect family dog. But whenever they took him on a hike and let him off leash, his true nature kicked in, and he'd be five mountain ranges away before he ever decided he might be a little tired and it was time to come back. They'd call and call for him, didn't matter. Blue just had to keep covering ground. Long legs and a big barrel chest—he was made to run. He couldn't help it. Then he'd finally show up back on the trail in front of them with his tongue hanging out, desperate for water, looking like he'd just had the greatest time."

"So what was he doing?" Amanda asked.

"No one knows. Chasing things? Just running? Flying? Who knows. My brother's friend finally put a GPS collar on him just to see where he actually went. I'm not kidding about the distance. Blue might have gone twenty-five miles while the family was hiking five." Winnie pointed with her water bottle before taking a sip. "That's you."

Amanda chomped another chip. She grinned. "Sounds right. Thank you, I'm flattered."

Winnie had been right in her assessment within the first few minutes of meeting Amanda Birkauer. They were meant to be friends. As different as they were in so many ways, they were also exactly the same in so many others.

They both had an unquenchable thirst for knowledge. They both knew that psychic abilities were real. They both knew that despite the scorn of the scientific community and the skepticism of the public, the powers of the human mind and the secrets of consciousness deserved to be explored and studied with as much commitment as people studied the stars and the galaxies and the human body.

Winnie and Amanda were both, in that way, like Blue the Shorthaired Pointer: made to explore. Made to keep going over that next horizon and the next. There might be something exciting over there. Let's go look. What's that? I saw something move. I'm going over there next.

I'll come back when I need water and I'm ready to rest.

In her regular daily life, Winnie had settled into a peaceful, easy routine, just her and her own first soulful dog. It had taken her a long time to find her footing again after Joe died three years ago, but she felt like she had a firm foundation underneath her now. She had found for herself the right balance among the things she still loved: her quiet home life, plenty of fresh air and lots of reading, regular visits with her brother's two adult children and their families, and plenty of other low-key and satisfying activities of daily living.

But Winnie's mind was still sharp and ever-hungry for knowledge. It was why being an academic had suited her for so many years. It was why marrying a man with a brilliant mind of his own had given her thirty-one years of joy.

And it was why Winnie always jumped at the chance now to visit Amanda Birkauer in her lab and see what new experiments the scientists there had been cooking up lately. Winnie met the most interesting people through Amanda, whether they were fellow parapsychologists eager to share their findings, or other psychic volunteers like Winnie who wanted to learn more about their own abilities.

She wasn't surprised Amanda had given her so little advance notice about this new parapsychology experiment, whatever it was. Winnie had told her over the years to surprise her. To keep information to herself and let Winnie come into it clean, without any bias or preconceived ideas.

So all Winnie knew as she walked back to campus in the gradually warming spring air was what Amanda had told her a few days before: that there would be British and Russian participants, and that at least some of them had impressive abilities.

Winnie didn't feel competitive—at least she sincerely

hoped not—but she did feel a sense of excitement. She had learned so much from other clairvoyants and mediums and intuitives over the years, and she knew her own abilities had started climbing once Amanda Birkauer starting challenging Winnie to do more.

If Amanda said this was going to be fun, Winnie knew she was telling the truth. Amanda didn't like to be bored, either. She always wanted to entertain her own ever-hungry mind.

Winnie's feet picked up the pace. This was not a time to stroll. Some kind of new discovery was waiting for her on campus. The sooner she got there, the sooner she'd find out exactly what it was.

4

As she made her way through the neighborhood toward the University of Arizona campus, Winnie passed the old homes where so many other fellow academics lived. A biology professor lived in that two-story with the enviable garden out front. The head of the pharmacology college lived in that old brick one-story with the nice wide porch out front with the Adirondack chairs. Winnie passed the corner house where a retired law school professor lived with her artist wife. They had some kind of tree out front that Winnie kept meaning to ask them about with leaves that actually turned yellow once the temperatures finally dipped. A little splash of fall color in a climate where normally the primary colors were brown and dusty green.

Even if she kept forgetting to ask them about the tree, Winnie knew that one day the answer would just pop into her head, like toast popping up from a toaster. That was how a lot of information showed up, and she enjoyed the surprise of it.

There were other dog-walkers out. Winnie knew by sight all the ones who usually walked when she and Clover and Arthur did, so she didn't tend to know this later crowd. But there was Emma, the two-year-old black Lab with a very calm and dignified disposition for a Lab that young. Emma was usually out early like Winnie and her pack.

Winnie waved to the woman walking her. She knew the woman's name was Carolyn, but she would never use it unless she had to. Usually the dog walkers only knew each other's dogs' names—and they knew all of them. "Well, who's this?" "This is Charlie." "Hi, Charlie! Are you having a nice walk?" Pet, sniff.

Whereas asking about their person's name was, by some unspoken but apparently universal code, considered uncool. As if they were breaking a thin wall of civilization that said they should only be known as Emma's mom and Clover's mom and Charlie's dad.

But of course Winnie knew all of the people's names. Her clairvoyance gave her all sorts of information, whether she sought it at that particular moment or not.

Names, occupations, relationships, troubles,

triumphs, secrets … at times Winnie intentionally blocked them all out and let herself enjoy an information-free walk, but over the years she had gathered quite a catalog of people's details that she had no particular need to know.

Carolyn liked to crochet, for example. Her husband broke his hand last year when he was running after a grandchild in their backyard and he tripped and fell. In addition to their sweet black Lab Emma, they had a cat named Jerome who was a biter and a scratcher. Emma was still trying hard to make the cat like her. It didn't look like she had a chance. Were any of these details important? Yes, to them, though not so much to Winnie. But she still knew those and so many other things. It was how her mind worked.

Winnie had long ago stopped feeling overwhelmed by the constant stream of information. When she was a child it was sometimes oppressive. But now, at sixty-eight, Winnie had a close and appreciative bond with her clairvoyant mind. She valued it as her closest friend and partner and treated it with as much love and respect as she could.

Carolyn called from across the street, "Where're the pups?"

Which was also the universal code. None of them should ever be out walking without their dogs.

"They already had their walks," Winnie called back.

Carolyn nodded. Order restored. No one was going to have to call the Dog Police on Winnie.

Winnie smiled to herself as she walked on. She loved her neighborhood, with all its set pieces of old houses and old trees and friendly people and happy dogs.

Sure, occasionally there would be roving bands of javelina and skinny, lurking coyotes that kept them all on the lookout and shouting warnings to each other so they could avoid any unfortunate interactions, but overall this was the best place Winnie had ever found to live, and she was grateful she still lived here.

And being just a few blocks from the university campus was definitely one of the perks.

Winnie crossed at the light and aimed her steps toward the Psychology building, ahead on her right.

It hadn't changed one bit on the outside from when she first began teaching there nearly forty years ago now. The exterior was all red brick. Solid and classic. The ground all around the building featured concrete sidewalks with graveled areas in between. Not exactly inspiring or a joy to behold.

But Winnie appreciated that some ambitious landscape designer decades ago had convinced the university to install raised brick planting beds all over campus to provide splashes of color and life.

The planter in front of the Psychology building showed off a rotating display of red and purple petunias and pansies, and yellow, pink, and white snapdragons, depending on the season. Some did better in winter, others when the temperatures rose until everyone was living inside an oven set to *Roast*.

Inside the building, nothing much had changed since Winnie's first days of teaching there. Like so many of the old buildings on campus, it smelled faintly of sweat and old books. The ceilings were still low, the lighting still a shade too dark, and any classroom or office that had a window was still a coveted prize. Bricks were obviously more economical than windows, and so any view outside, even if it was only of the exterior stairwell, felt both rare and precious.

Professors who achieved one of those offices or classrooms usually took full advantage by shoving tables up against the windows and crowding potted plants everywhere they could.

Winnie had done that herself. It took eleven years, but the day she moved into an office with a window looking out on the sidewalk in front of the building, she made sure to bring in half a dozen pots filled with geraniums, a sprawling golden pothos, and cheerful little violets to instantly make herself feel at home.

While much of the building looked exactly as it did when Winnie first accepted her teaching job here, the one thing that had changed—and very much for the better—was the lab space down in the basement. When Winnie participated in the fateful experiment when she met Joe, there were only a few small rooms dedicated to exploration.

Now, under the leadership of Dr. Amanda Birkauer and her boss Dr. Kuhlman, the entire north wing of the basement had been redesigned and renovated to include large open spaces that held the latest brain measuring equipment and allowed for large groups of scientists and participants to spread out and feel comfortable.

There were also smaller nooks, the size of walk-in closets, with copper-lined walls or outfitted as Faraday cages to screen out potential electromagnetic interference from the environment and allow for isolated measurements of human energetic fields and brain activity.

All of it real science. All of it, to Winnie's mind, beyond exciting. She never could have dreamed of any of this when she was a little girl frightened by the colors she saw around people and by the words and images that flooded into her young mind. No one she knew saw the world the way she did. No one ever spoke about knowing things about people without learning them in the conventional ways. Her mother and her friends might gossip about a neighbor they thought was dishonest or unfaithful or who stole money from the church donation box—but Winnie always knew with certainty the things other people tried to keep hidden.

It was a curse at times, an ability she wished she didn't have.

But it was also a blessing that had saved Winnie, her brother, and her parents from more than a few disasters over the years. Like the time Winnie screamed at her father to hit the brakes, "RIGHT NOW!" and he did it, because he knew his daughter, and he knew there had to be a reason.

It was late at night on a dark country road where they were driving home from a cousin's wedding.

It had rained all day. Mud caked their tires, making it hard for Winnie's father to steer.

Twelve-year-old Winnie had been dozing in the back seat next to her older brother when suddenly the image popped into her mind: the bridge they had crossed in the daylight, the bridge that was just around the bend ahead of them, had washed out some time in the last hour, and there would be no way to see that in the dark before it was too late.

They would have rounded the curve and driven straight into the raging river. All of them would certainly have drowned.

The family got out where Winnie's father braked to a halt, and he brought the flashlight out of the glove compartment to see why on earth Winnie had screamed to stop.

The four of them stood at a safe distance from the

crumbling bank and stared at what would have taken their lives.

Winnie's father put his arm around her shoulders.

"Well done," he said.

Winnie's mother was more demonstrative, giving her a full hug and kissing the top of her head.

Even fourteen-year-old Steven managed a casual, "Yeah, thanks," even though Winnie could hear the fear in his voice.

Her family never treated her like a freak—although they didn't talk about Winnie's gifts in public. It was their family's secret. That was fine with Winnie. She didn't want to advertise it, either.

In time she learned to accept—and finally appreciate—that her clairvoyance and occasional precognition and other psychic skills were part of her, as much as having green eyes and being right-handed and not being able to curl her tongue the way Steven could. It was all just part of the overall package of being Winifred Elizabeth Taylor. Named after her grandmother and her mother's favorite movie star.

Winnie weaved through groups of students entering and exiting the building. It had been four years since she retired, and unless she ran into a grad student who had once taken one of her classes, Winnie never expected to be recognized. And that was fine with her. As much as she used to love teaching and interacting with her students, she was content now to be an anonymous older-looking lady dressed casually and not doing anything important. No need to look over here.

Winnie trotted down the stairs into the basement. Her heart was beating a little faster than normal in anticipation of a fun treat.

The last time she had been at the mind lab, Winnie participated in an experiment to see whether she and the other volunteers could influence Petri dishes full of live yogurt cultures to organize in specific patterns that could be seen under the microscope. Winnie picked a pattern like the one in her grandmother's quilt she had hanging on her bedroom wall behind the headboard. Each quilting square held a six-sided center piece surrounded by two outer circles made up of those same shapes in different fabrics. Winnie couldn't duplicate the colors, but she concentrated hard on organizing the cultures into those shapes.

After Amanda and her lab assistants analyzed the results, they emailed all the participants the various patterns everyone had made.

It was like looking through a kaleidoscope. Each volunteer had created a completely different pattern, but taken all together, the yogurt cultures looked like one cohesive display, something Winnie could imagine seeing in a modern art gallery some day.

Amanda surprised the volunteers by making T-shirts with their own designs on them. Winnie still had hers. It was too wild to wear out in public, even if it did look like a granny's quilt, but Winnie loved wearing it as a knock-around shirt around the house.

Winnie swung open the door to the largest lab space. Instead of gas burners and sinks and other accouterments of chemistry and biology labs, this one had rows of Scandinavian-style tables with black metal bases and light pine tops. The mind lab looked clean and sleek and modern.

Over the years Amanda Birkauer and her boss had made lots of contacts among wealthy people interested in the work they were doing. Business titans and investors might not want to be public about their curiosity, but they were more than willing to support explorations into psychic phenomena anonymously.

Since Winnie herself had spent years as an anonymous test subject while teaching in the same Psychology building on the floor above, she understood the desire for privacy.

One of the mind lab's supporters had approached Amanda a few years ago about donating an entire office floor's worth of furniture they were replacing during a redesign. Amanda was happy to ditch the old mismatched hand-me-downs she'd used to furnish this large lab space and some of the smaller test rooms, and replace them with desks and tables and chairs that were actually comfortable and soothing on the eyes.

Depending on the experiments, Amanda and her

lab assistants could seat people together at the same long conference tables, or, like they'd done today, put up temporary movable dividers along the tables that created private nooks where people could sit across from each other for experiments.

Cameras had been set up in strategic places throughout the room to record experiments from various angles: from the sides, above looking down, and some aimed at each chair to capture individual responses at the same time.

Winnie had learned to tune out the cameras and all the other equipment Amanda Birkauer used: instruments that measured volunteers' brain waves, respiration rates, heart rates, and other vitals during experiments. The results were always fascinating to hear about, but Winnie didn't want to be self-conscious about her body's internal workings while her mind explored Amanda's tests.

The mind lab always felt good to come into. Amanda made sure the lighting and furnishings made it feel welcome. And it helped that everywhere there was a window, even though they were slim and high up because of the lab's placement down in the basement, plants in colorful pots climbed and spread and thrived.

Winnie hesitated just inside the doorway. She didn't expect to be the first one there, but already the crowd was larger than she expected.

Around the perimeter of the room, in groups of

twos and threes, stood about a dozen or more strangers. Winnie could feel her old shyness kicking in. She never felt this way about meeting new people one-on-one. In fact, she usually enjoyed it. People's lives and personalities were so interesting. Winnie liked to know how they thought.

But no matter how old she was, or how many different social situations she had been in throughout the course of her life, Winnie still felt her familiar childhood nervousness about walking into a room and not knowing anyone.

At least this wasn't one of the situations when everyone stopped talking and turned to look at her. That was the worst. It brought back memories of a few disastrous sleepovers when she was young.

She had experienced this same unwelcome shyness every single semester for all the years—the decades—of her teaching career, every time she walked into her classroom or a lecture hall on the first day.

Even though she felt completely confident in her subject. Even though she'd already taught thousands of students. Even though she knew that by her second class with all of them, she would feel normal and comfortable again.

She still braced herself for that moment when all those faces turned to her, looked her over, wondered what she was like and what she would say.

She still paused in the doorway each time and

looked out on the sea of new people and saw the swirls of their auras around them, the colors telling her who was eager, who was bored, who would be trouble, who would be a delight. Then she'd turn down the dial on her perception and walk to the front of the room, smile, and launch into her prepared introduction.

Knowing she would get through it. But still dreading those first words she had to be brave enough to speak.

"Hello, everyone, welcome. I'm Professor Parsons." And before that, Professor Taylor. Neither announcement especially controversial. No one was going to object, cry out, stand up and storm out. But Winnie's palms still sweated through those first moments of every single first class, and she simply learned to take it in stride.

At least by now, this many years into her habit, she could smile at herself for what she felt. She had great compassion for the shy little girl she had been, and for the grown older woman she was now. She had no need to bully or berate herself. Instead, she just gave herself as much time as she needed to acclimate. Like a diver ascending from the deep.

From just inside the mind lab doorway now, Winnie surveyed the group of strangers laughing and chatting with each other. Even though they were strangers to Winnie, they weren't to each other.

A few of them had looked over at her as she entered

the room. A natural reaction, since she was a stranger, too. But then they had resumed their conversations. Winnie could feel herself relax. Everything was fine. And Amanda promised this would be fun.

Winnie saw Amanda now at the far end of the lab, waving her arm to Winnie high enough to be seen over people's heads. Amanda wore her standard uniform of University of Arizona athletic clothes: navy blue running pants with the Wildcat emblem on the left leg, sneakers, and a long-sleeved gray T-shirt with *UA Mind Lab* in navy print. No baseball cap this time, but her long brown and graying hair was still pulled back into a high ponytail. Winnie had never seen her wear makeup. Amanda always looked naturally healthy and hearty.

Winnie weaved through the small crowd, smiling at the men and women as she passed. She caught snippets of their accents: British here, British there, everywhere a Brit.

She relaxed even more. Everything was going to be fine.

Amanda stood next to a thin, dark-haired woman wearing black leggings, black ankle boots, and a purple hoodie with Princeton on front. She was in her early thirties, Winnie guessed—a voice in her mind said *thirty-three*—with eyes so dark they were almost black. She had dark eyebrows, too, darker than her chin-length sable hair, making her face seem even paler than it probably was. Her features had both a delicate and hard look to them, as if a master sculptor had carved her beauty out of ice.

"Irina," Amanda said, pronouncing it *Ee-ree-na*, "this is my friend Winnie."

And then the ice melted as the woman offered Winnie a genuine and luminous smile. Irina stuck out her hand and gave Winnie a surprisingly strong handshake.

"I am very pleased to meet you," Irina said, and Winnie had the feeling the woman really meant it. As if she might already know a few things about Winnie, and had been waiting and eager to meet her.

Which shouldn't be a surprise: either Amanda had told her something about Winnie, or Irina was one of the people with "impressive skills," and she knew a few things on her own.

There was something else: the accent.

"Yes, Russian," Irina answered, even though Winnie didn't ask. "But friendly," she said, smiling again.

Winnie couldn't remember ever meeting someone with such a relaxed and sincere and—what could she call it? *Complete*—smile. As if all of Irina's life were fun to her. As if living itself was fun.

Her smile felt infectious. Winnie couldn't help smiling back.

"I've paired you up this morning," Amanda told Winnie. "So don't talk about anything yet. I just wanted you to get the first awkwardness over. No time for that."

Winnie took it as she knew Amanda meant it: not as ridicule, but as understanding. Amanda knew about Winnie's shyness in a group and always did her best to help her get past it.

"Everyone," Amanda shouted over the lively chatter in the lab. "Take your last pee breaks. Fun starts in five."

She left Winnie and Irina and went to confer with her two lab assistants who were busy setting up their equipment.

"I always go even if I don't have to," Irina said. "Just telling me I can't makes me feel more urgent."

She smiled at her own quirk and then began threading her way through the crowd, in somewhat of a hurry. Apparently she wasn't exaggerating.

Now that the initial shyness was behind her, Winnie could look around the room with greater leisure. Maybe half of the people had followed Amanda's suggestion and left in search of a restroom. Winnie now counted seven men and women she didn't know.

She did recognize the two lab assistants. They were grad students who routinely worked for Amanda in the mind lab. Winnie waved to one who caught her eye.

The grad student, Vella, came toward her carrying a handful of wires. She wore an oversized black T-shirt with the mind lab logo on it, and a pair of jeans that looked uncomfortably tight on her curvy body. Winnie always felt tempted to take girls aside and tell them they didn't have to wear things that pinched, hurt, that they had to suck in to zip up—none of it. Winnie knew from experience. She used to torture herself in clothing, too. Then one day it finally occurred to her how insane that practice was. She weeded out and gave away a whole wardrobe of clothing that didn't fit right, and had never looked back. She wished Vella and everyone else could find that same kind of freedom.

But Winnie had to accept that today was probably not that day.

"Hello, Professor."

"Hi, Vella, how are you?"

Vella gave a little groan. "Stressed. Some of this stuff isn't working. Can I try one on you?"

"Sure." Winnie stood still while Vella pulled what felt like a plastic headband over her scalp, finally settling it across Winnie's forehead and angling back. The ends of the headband were slightly curved to fit around her ears. Wires trailed behind. She felt like she was wearing a long wig.

Vella fiddled with the dial in her hand, attached to the wires. Winnie could see red and green lights taking turns to flash.

"Okay, I got it," Vella said. She helped Winnie remove the headband, only pulling a few of her hairs in the process. "Whoops, sorry … sorry!"

Winnie chuckled. "Won't be the first time. I'm sure Dr. Birkauer has a whole collection of hair somewhere. I've been donating it for twenty-five years."

Vella smiled uncertainly, maybe not convinced Winnie was kidding.

As hard working and brilliant as Winnie had found this latest lab assistant of Amanda's to be, Vella did seem to lack a humor chip. Or maybe she was just always afraid she might get it wrong if she laughed at something one of the professors said.

Although Vella might have had a glint in her eye just now as she fished out another one of Winnie's white hairs from the wires and handed it to its owner. "She'll never get this one," Vella said seriously, as if she and Winnie were conspiring.

Irina was still off on her personal errand. Winnie stood alone as she listened to the pair of volunteers nearest her.

Their lovely English accents. She could listen to them all day long. Even if they were just reading a list of school supplies or talking about garden mulch. Didn't matter. Something about the beautiful sound of it transported her to green hillsides and white cliffs towering above a cold ocean shore. Winnie could imagine wearing a thick fisherman's sweater and a heavy yellow rain slicker over it, and big black rubber boots, and calling out in her own English accent, "Pull 'er in! Now! Godssake! Hurry!"

Winnie's eyes jerked open. She didn't realize she'd closed them.

She could see dark-haired Irina making her way back toward her. In the restroom Irina had pulled back the sides of her hair into a clip, exposing even more of her pale, chiseled face. She looked ready to work. Ready to play. Her smile said as much.

Amanda Birkauer gave a loud clap of her hands. "All right! Let's get started. We have a full morning. You all have your partners. Grab your seats and we'll hook you up."

"This looks good," Irina said, indicating the chairs closest to them, at the end of the long pine-topped table.

She and Winnie were just taking their seats when a man Winnie hadn't noticed before stepped behind Irina and whispered something in her ear. He was dark-haired and handsome, with a tan, healthy-looking complexion. He wore jeans and sneakers and a red T-shirt under a black hoodie. His eyes were black like Irina's.

Winnie wondered for a moment if this was Irina's boyfriend, until Irina batted the man away like a fly, not caring at all that she actually made contact and backhanded him in the face. Winnie gasped. She couldn't help it. That backhand looked like it hurt.

But the man grinned at Winnie, proving he was unharmed—and unoffended. He said something to

Irina in what sounded like Russian, and went off to take his own seat.

Irina noticed Winnie's look of surprise.

"Twin study," Irina said with a shrug. "My little brother by two minutes. They keep inviting us both. When will they learn." The words sounded cynical, but her smile was warm. Irina obviously liked her brother.

It was another point in her favor. Winnie had liked her brother, too.

When they were young Steven liked to try to get her in trouble by making her laugh when she shouldn't. Church services, school ceremonies, anywhere where they supposed to behave. He'd mumble so quietly, only Winnie could hear him. *Keep a straight face. It isn't funny. I think he just farted. Don't breathe in.*

Winnie wondered what Irina's twin whispered to her just now. Whatever it was, Winnie admired the backhand. It never occurred to her to respond in any way except laughing.

"Listen up!" Amanda called over the chattering in the room. "We're going to make you do some magic today. Get ready to be amazed."

5

Winnie's colleague Bernadine seemed nervous as she set up the test.

But handsome Air Force Major Joe Parsons was not.

Winnie could barely look at him across the scarred wooden table. All of the furniture down there looked like it came from a garage sale. Or maybe it was the dregs of some other department, maybe something destined for the trash, but good enough for the parapsychology lab. No one wanted to fund it. Most of the faculty thought it was an embarrassment. Winnie had seen good work done by Bernadine and her fellow brave researchers, but the lab still seemed to be held together by chicken wire and duct tape and spit. Like a cheap craft project someone still needed to create, if only to express what was in their mind.

Winnie kept her legs bent, feet well behind her underneath her rickety metal chair, for fear she might accidentally kick Major Parsons's long legs.

Every time she risked looking at him, he smiled. It was unnerving.

Because Winnie could imagine something else:

Joe Parsons reaching across that table with his right hand up, gently waiting for Winnie to place her left hand in his.

This complete stranger, Joe Parsons, slipping a gold band onto Winnie's left finger, left hand, then closing his warm fingers over hers.

And telling her, *I love you. I will love you the rest of our lives.*

Then Winnie's brain would clear and there was her friend Bernadine nervously fiddling with the video camera while Joe Parsons patiently waited for the experiment to begin and even more patiently waited for Winnie's gaze to meet his.

It was maddening. Winnie wanted to do it. She resisted like she was the iron filings trying to fight against the force of a magnet.

At last, although maybe it had only been five minutes. Or maybe three or two, but it felt like so much longer.

At last Winnie gave in and looked up into Joe

Parsons's warm brown eyes, and she smiled and she finally relaxed.

Because he knew it, too. Somehow, some way, even though he claimed not to have an ounce of clairvoyant ability himself.

He had come to the parapsychology lab that day in an act of defiance against his general.

Or at least that was why Joe thought he was there. Until he met Winnie. And knew, he told her later, within the first thirty seconds.

"How?" she asked him, letting her fingers intertwine with his as she leaned back against him on his slipcovered couch and listened to a Bonnie Raitt song play in the background.

They had been dating for two weeks. Fourteen nights in a row. The last four of them, sleepovers. Winnie was amazed they resisted that long.

Not because they burned with a passion so hot—although Winnie never, in her life, had felt so attracted to someone as she did to Joe—but because they could feel it from that very first day: the light and the warmth and the comfort of absolute belonging. The sense of rightness about it, even though logic wanted to intrude. *What are you doing? You just met! You can't possibly feel like this.*

But Winnie did. And Joe did. And that was just how it was.

So they gave up any resistance. Including resistance

to the fact that they were meant to be together every night from then on.

Winnie knew how she knew. The images had flooded her mind as she stood out in the hallway that Saturday, trying to decide whether to go back into the room or run away.

Bonnie Raitt's song played softly in the background. There was an ache to it. The pain of loving someone who did not love her.

Winnie felt the opposite.

"How?" she asked Joe. How did he know?

The back of her head rested against his chest as they stretched together across his couch. She could feel him breathing, steady and relaxed. Her fingers curled around his.

Major Parsons tapped his chest. Winnie could feel the movement and hear the soft thud.

"It's what they train us to do," he said. "To act before you're certain why you know. They won't call it intuition—that's too soft. They call it *pilot's nose*. It's that sudden knowing that you have to turn your plane. Or check your instruments. Or respond to whatever just creeped into your chest. You know something's wrong. You have to fix it before you understand what it is. By then, it's going to be too late. You're dead."

Winnie had laughed. "Well. That sounds romantic."

Joe squeezed her hand. Hugged his arms a little

tighter around her. Held her, cherished her, in a way she had never experienced in her life.

"If I didn't nab you," Joe told her, "it was going to be all over." He imitated the sound of a plane going down. "I didn't know why, but I sure knew I was right."

Winnie knew he was right, too. Even though it scared her, how fast and how deep their love grew. She kept thinking it couldn't last. It couldn't keep getting better. But it did, and it did.

She had done what she set out to do in Bernadine's experiment. Winnie had deliberately failed at every single test. She proved that she had zero psychic ability, and that Bernadine's experiment itself was flawed beyond repair. Because her only other test subject that day, Major Parsons, thought it was more important to win himself a girlfriend than to stick to the experiment protocol.

Midway through the test, while the video camera was rolling, while Bernadine was faithfully taking notes of everything her two parapsychology subjects were saying, Joe stopped cooperating. There was no point to it—none at all. He knew by then, *pilot's nose*, that his decision the day before on what he thought was impulse to volunteer for an experiment at the parapsychology lab wasn't, in fact, the reason he had to be there.

The woman sitting across from him was the reason.

He could explore the other phenomenon—the inexplicable and maybe even mystical experience he had had while on a flight seven months before—some other time. Some other day. All of his training and his intuition told him he had to act now, or he would regret it the rest of his life.

"Please," he asked Winnie. "Would you come with me now?" Joe was supposed to be looking at one of the Zener cards and sending her an image of what he saw, but that meant nothing to his life. This did.

Winnie wondered if she was still breathing. And whether Joe and Bernadine could hear her heart pounding, the way it sounded in her own hears, like a dozen drums all beating at once.

She wasn't a teenager anymore, but her heart sure got that wrong. The way it sped up, the way her head felt too light, the way her palms sweated and her whole body felt swoony as if the boy she had always liked just asked her to the prom.

Winnie didn't trust her voice. It would probably crack. She knew her cheeks were flushed and her green eyes were probably wide with what looked like fear.

But it wasn't fear. It was knowledge. She had already seen where all this would lead. The images had flooded through her mind as Winnie stood out in the hallway gathering her courage to go back in.

So she nodded. And smiled. And Joe held out his hand to her and they got up and left together.

Bernadine was not happy. Bernadine shouted at them to come back.

But it was too late. They had already stepped onto the ride together.

They married three months later, on another Saturday, this one in January. And they remained married for thirty-one years. Not, as Joe had promised her, for the rest of their lives, but certainly for his. Winnie wanted more—more time, more love—but she was grateful for every single day that she got.

And grateful for that midnight flight Joe had been on seven months before when suddenly his instruments went wild, everything around him went black, and his plane hit the surface of the black ocean and broke in half and immediately began to sink.

He should have died. He thought he did.

It happened so quickly, he didn't have a chance to suck a breath in before he sank.

So his lungs were empty. The water was shockingly —deathly—cold. He was still strapped into his seat.

Habit overcame panic and he reached with his right arm to release the buckle on the seatbelt. But the arm was useless. The impact had shattered the ball of his right shoulder.

Still without air, he fumbled with his left hand, now numb with cold, and somehow got the belt loose.

But the plane—the half he was still inside, open to the water and sinking like an anchor—was so deep under the surface by now, there was no way Joe could swim to the top before he drowned.

Even if he weren't so deep, even if he had managed to take a breath before he sank, there was still no way he could do it with only one good arm.

The night had been clear and black. Perfect for flying. Joe had feasted his eyes on the stars as he followed the flight path he had been told to take.

There were other pilots taking other flight paths that night, testing the same model of plane that had broken apart on Joe.

Now, deep under the cold and killing sea, Joe's lungs could no longer bear being empty. They begged Joe to breathe again. Even if all he could breath in was water.

And his body told him to move—to try it, try *anything*—even if only one arm was working.

Joe knew he was about to die. Might already be dead, for all he knew. Everything felt slow and cold and dark and absolutely unreal.

Up above him, far in the distance, he saw a blinking white light.

Part of his brain, too frigid to think logically anymore, still knew that what he was seeing couldn't really be there.

He was a trained diver. He had been on plenty of dives before. He knew as deep as he was, no light could reach him. No light could possibly be visible from where he was.

But his body didn't seem to care. His mind didn't seem to care. The light was there, it was blinking, it was beckoning him: *Come swim.*

With only his left arm able to pull him through the water, with not an ounce of air in his lungs, Joe's body took over and made him swim toward the light. Made his legs kick. And keep kicking. No matter how impossibly far they had to go. Made his heart keep beating, pumping the last of any oxygen up to his brain. And made his lungs wait and keep waiting, even though they were screaming for air, begging him to breathe, telling him they had nothing more to give.

He made it to the surface. He had no idea how. All of it was unquestionably impossible.

And then Joe disappeared from his life while he took his first gasps of air.

All around him he saw the stars.

Not just one blinking and beckoning him to it.

But a whole skyful of them, surrounding him like a shimmering blanket, covering him with warmth and light.

He floated now, not on the cold dark ocean, but on a bed of warm, glowing stars. Comfortable and safe. And, he realized, dead.

It meant nothing to him. There was no struggle anymore. No bodily imperative to do anything. He had already done it. He'd gotten free of the seatbelt, free of the plane, and he'd swum toward the blinking light.

Nothing more was required of him, he knew that. And he couldn't have done any more anyway. He was completely drained of any and all energy. Of energy and will. He had no more will to live or die or do anything except simply exist on this comfortable bed of light.

Time meant nothing. He might have floated like that for hours or days or years. It didn't matter. Time was irrelevant. Joe just rested and let it all go.

He wasn't even waiting for anything. What was there to wait for? He'd already died. This was what it was.

And then a hand grabbed his wrist.

And the night came back. And the freezing water. And the frigid gusts of wind. And the searing pain in his right shoulder and other pain throughout his whole body.

"Major? Major!"

Then the recovery team took him out of the ocean and back into life and everything else resumed its normal course. Hospitals, debriefings, recovery—

And an experience that Joe now needed to understand for himself.

Did he die that night? He did. He knew it at a basic, hollowed-out level. He could try to logic it away, try to tell himself he didn't know what he knew—but Major

Parsons was a lover of facts and reason, and he wouldn't lie to himself.

He couldn't talk about it. Not to anyone. Who would believe him? Who would want to hear it?

He was rock solid, reliable, a leader and a mentor. If he told anyone what happened, they would think he was cracking up. That they couldn't trust him anymore. That he needed help of some kind, when really Joe knew he just needed to understand.

But it had changed him, he knew that, too. He couldn't move through his life with the same surface detachment he used to have.

Now everything felt serious and important. But also, surprisingly light. A veil had fallen away, one he didn't realize had been in front of him his whole life, and now he saw things with a clearer, deeper eye.

It seemed to smooth away sharp edges people were used to him having. What was the point of getting irritated by small mistakes those around him made? What was the point of pushing himself to be perfect, when how he was doing everything was fine as it was?

He wasn't depressed. He didn't feel hopeless. That wasn't it at all. He hadn't lost the will to live.

It was just that he saw his life in a different way— saw *all* life differently. The things that used to seem so essential didn't mean much at all to him anymore.

Whether he advanced in the Air Force. He would or he wouldn't. Whether he pleased his superiors. Joe was an honest, competent man in every category of his life. He knew that. He wouldn't pretend he didn't. And either that was enough for his superiors and his friends and everyone else in his life, or it wasn't. But this was who he was and that was good enough for him.

It was as if he had left all striving and ambition down under the cold dark water of the sea. It was enough to be alive. He had survived. He had died and now here he was again, and how he led his life from now on seemed like a fresh and open road.

But he still wondered. Of course he did. He had an inquisitive, analytical mind. He searched through bookstores for any memoirs of people who went through something like he did.

A nurse on a medical flight in Alaska who was the sole survivor when the plane crashed into a remote lake. She, too, suffered injuries that should have meant it was impossible for her to swim. But while she watched her body in the water from some vantage up above it, she saw herself swimming despite a broken leg, broken pelvis, and fractured collar bone. The real her, the one watching from someplace above, felt no pain, no effort, as she watched the drama below.

Then once her body crawled onto shore, she felt herself rush back into it. And felt the pain that went along with it.

Joe read about a mountain climber who fell into a crevasse along with his climbing partner, who died.

The man was sure he must have died, too. He spent the next day or more outside his body while he watched himself struggle to climb back out, to free himself, despite not just one, but two broken legs.

Joe realized he had gotten off easy with just his shattered shoulder. But the stories he read sounded so familiar to him, it was as if the writers were describing his own thoughts and even the periods of no thinking at all that Joe could still conjure back for himself whenever he remembered everything he experienced that night.

But he needed more. Not just survival stories, but explanations. He was grateful to know he was not the only one, but he still didn't know what to make of it. How was he supposed to integrate it into his continuing life?

And then came the directive from his superior, General Nash. Apparently some flyer had made the rounds on base, inviting anyone who was interested in learning about psychic phenomena and extrasensory abilities to come volunteer for a study at the University of Arizona parapsychology lab.

General Nash made it clear that no one under his command would be participating in something like that. Joe read the general's words: *fantasy, sham, preying on weak minds.*

But Joe knew his mind was sharp and strong.

And here, maybe, he could find answers.

He found a copy of the banned flyer and saw there was an experiment taking place the following morning. He was off on Saturdays. His time was his own.

His life was his own. Hadn't he lost it, then somehow gotten it back?

He could do with it what he chose. An unpopular attitude if he wanted to advance and even remain in the military, but Joe couldn't unknow what he knew.

So he presented himself as a volunteer at the university the next morning.

And met the love of his life.

Who eventually led him to the answers he needed. But that was still a year away, as Winnie patiently practiced hypnosis to help him explore the deepest caverns of his mind.

And in the meantime, the two of them got to enjoy their first year of marriage. On the way to thirty more after that.

Winnie helped Joe confirm that yes, he had died that night. And yes, he had been saved. Both, in reverse order. Survival, death, survival.

Why, he never knew, although Winnie told him it might be as simple as the fact that Major Joe Parsons—later, Colonel Joe Parsons—was a good man. And the world needed good men and women. It didn't mean all of them got to survive—Winnie knew good people died all the time. And even the ones who did survive didn't get to live forever. That much, Winnie also understood, even though she wished with all her heart it wasn't true.

And of course the reverse was also true. Wicked people got to live, sometimes well into old age. There had to be a reason. Some sort of cosmic balancing that even with her clairvoyance, Winnie couldn't see.

But needing more good people in this world might be at least one simple reason why sometimes people defied death and squeezed out another portion of life.

The nurse on a medical flight. A mountain climber. A pilot in a crashed plane.

Joe's answers would one day come, but he didn't know any of that when he sat in the basement of the Psychology building at a little wooden table and gazed at the professor sitting across from him.

He only knew what he felt. Pilot's heart.

"This isn't going to work," he told the researcher who kept prodding them to answer questions that meant nothing to Joe. He could feel his impatience rising. He was wasting time—they both were.

"What do you mean?" the woman conducting the tests asked. Joe had forgotten her name. He knew she was a professor, just like the volunteer sitting across from him, but nothing else mattered at the moment except making sure the woman across from him wouldn't get away.

"I'm sorry, I don't get any of this," Joe said. He set down the cards and removed the sensors the researcher had attached to his temples and his heart. "I apologize, but this isn't working."

Winnie had sat so perfectly still, afraid he was about to leave. Not believing that he could—she felt it. But nothing was going the way she expected.

"Please," Joe said, holding out his hand to Winnie. "Would you come with me now?"

Bernadine couldn't believe it. "No, she can't come with you. We're doing a test!"

Winnie couldn't help it. She felt both elated and foolish. Like someone was telling her to skip school. Come on. Let's go play.

Part of her knew she should have run away when she first saw him. This was dangerous. This man was going to upend her safe, predictable life.

But the better part—her heart, her clairvoyant mind—knew she was in safe hands. So she accepted that hand. Took off the sensors, just like Joe had, and made her apologies to her colleague.

"Winnie! Do you know how much all this costs?"

Winnie could guess. She knew it was hard to get any funding for anything but the most middle-of-the-road research. She felt for her colleague—she did.

But not enough not to leave with Joe Parsons and never look back.

There were consequences, of course. For Bernadine, for the parapsychology lab, for Winnie and

Bernadine's friendship, which never survived past that Saturday.

But Winnie could have told Bernadine from the start: *Oh, this is why we're here. That's the man I'm going to marry. Thank you, Bernadine, but let's all save ourselves the trouble. This experiment is over. And it's a success. Thank you from the bottom of my heart.*

And now Winnie was back in the lab, a place that had been upgraded and renewed, and though Joe Parsons wasn't here to make Winnie's heart pound again and hold out his hand to her and offer her the adventure of her lifetime, Winnie could still find joy in delving into the mysteries of the mind. With her friend Amanda, with this new partner, the Russian twin Irina, and with herself. Winnie's own inquisitive mind thrilled at the idea of learning something new.

NBB. Never Be Bored.

Winnie was ready to do some magic.

6

"These are wheat berry seeds," Amanda told them all as Vella and the other grad student lab assistant, a reserved young man named Geoffrey, went person to person handing out a little baggie filled with what looked like a moist paper towel folded in half.

Amanda and her assistants had already gone through the fiddly effort of outfitting all of the volunteers with the plastic headbands. Now everyone looked like they belonged to the same long-haired rock group with wires cascading down their backs. The older gentlemen with noticeably thinning hair looked particularly distinguished.

Winnie and Irina sat across from each other at the end of one of the long pine-topped tables. This one was open, without any dividers, so they could all see each other. Winnie counted sixteen volunteers total, sitting in eight pairs.

Irina's twin, whose name Winnie now knew was Max, had been paired with one of the balding hair-band members from England. Taken in isolation, the Brit's face seemed very serious and scholarly, but every time Winnie caught sight of his long wire wig it was hard for her not to laugh. Max seemed to know she found it hilarious, because he caught Winnie's eye and grinned. He seemed as fun-loving as his sister.

Not everyone looked ridiculous. In fact, Irina looked like Cleopatra, at least the version Elizabeth Taylor played in the movie where she fell in love with her future husband, Richard Burton. In the movie, her headdress had been made of strands of golden beads that hung down on her black hair and framed her gorgeous face. Irina had that kind of movie star glamour, Winnie realized, even without Elizabeth Taylor's heavy makeup, and dressed as she was like a plain student or faculty from Princeton.

And then Winnie got a flash. It happened sometimes, when she met someone new. An image or a mini-movie coming to Winnie's mind to show her a scene from that person's life.

Winnie saw Irina in a hospital bed. Her face looked drained of blood. Her whole body looked drained of life. Irina's lips were pale, nearly white. Her twin brother Max stood beside her clasping tightly to her hand. Crying, Winnie saw. The poor boy. They both looked younger, maybe by five or six years. Sometime in their late twenties.

A nurse came in. She said something to Max that Winnie couldn't hear, but she felt certain it was in English, not Russian. Max nodded. He seemed to swallow the lump in his throat.

"Will she…" Tears rained down Max's cheeks. He swallowed again, squeezed his twin sister's hand even harder, then spoke with a noticeably Russian accent. "Will she live?"

The nurse smiled and patted Max's arm. But that was the only answer she gave. Maybe the only one she could give.

To Winnie's eyes, it looked like Irina was close to dying.

It wasn't a scene Winnie wanted to watch.

Even though she knew Irina survived it, Winnie didn't want to see any more of this suffering she and Max had to go through.

Winnie purposely ended the mini-movie. She met Irina's dark gaze across from her.

Irina smiled and reached for Winnie's hands. "Tell me. What did you see?"

Winnie knew there was no point in denying it.

They were in the parapsychology lab. If they couldn't be honest here, where could they?

"You almost died."

"I did," Irina confirmed. Her smile lit up her face. "Isn't it wonderful?" She squeezed both Winnie's hands. "I have never tasted my life the same way again. I can tell you, it is *delicious*."

Winnie smiled at the description. She could believe this happy young woman got the most she could out of her life—especially after being so sick. Winnie would have loved to hear her talk more about it, but Irina had already moved on.

"Now," she told Winnie, releasing her hands, "let us tend to our little seeds."

Irina had such a mothering quality. A nurturer. She made Winnie feel calm and secure in her presence. Winnie felt like this young woman was somehow older and wiser than she was. An old soul. An old mother. Someone, Winnie realized, she could learn from, when based on their ages and experience, Winnie assumed she might have been the teacher.

But Irina was right. They had to pay attention to their experiment.

Amanda's instructions shortly before then had seemed simple. Each small plastic bag contained about a quarter cup of wheat berry seeds kept moist between the folds of a wet paper towel.

Winnie had never seen wheat berry seeds before. They looked like tiny little loaves of bread. Plump, like Rice Krispies, but smaller, the size of sunflower kernels outside their shells. They were light brown, with a darker brown line down the center of one side, the way a baker would cut into the top of a loaf of dough to release steam while it baked.

A few of the seeds had a dot of white on one of their ends. Winnie assumed that was where the seeds would sprout—if they did. She had zero experience with something like this. She loved plants and grew many of them from seed, but never the way Amanda had come up with for this experiment.

"These are your babies today," Amanda told them. "You are to love them, talk to them, feel toward them, and help them sprout … in the next ten minutes."

Everyone laughed.

But Winnie could feel the excitement in the room. Ten minutes? That was the kind of immediate gratification everyone wanted. If they were going to do magic, as Amanda Birkauer promised, let it be fast magic. Let's prove it.

"Pour your little babies into your palm," Amanda told them. "Your choice which hand. Then lay your other hand gently on top of them. Keep a nice, light touch."

Amanda demonstrated. "Not this," she said, clapping her hands together and potentially smooshing the little seeds. "Gently…" She brought her hands together as if cupping a little baby bird between them.

"We'll be monitoring your brain waves," Amanda said. "So don't hold back. Send your thoughts, your love, whatever you think will tell these little seeds to go ahead and grow.

"And no peeking," Amanda told them. "We'll all reveal at the same time. Ready? Your ten minutes starts … now."

Come on, my little friends, let's grow now. Come on, little seeds, grow for Mama…

Winnie felt a little silly sending her loving, encouraging thoughts to the seeds, but Amanda had been right: it was fun. Winnie kept catching herself laughing.

Irina laughed easily, too. In between she cooed to the seeds, she hummed a pretty song, she brought her hands up to her mouth and whispered gentle Russian endearments. Winnie kept forgetting to talk to her own seeds. She wanted to watch what Irina was doing.

"Five minutes!" Amanda called out. She and the lab assistants walked from pair to pair, watching, listening, smiling. The experiment was irresistible. Everyone was smiling.

"One more minute!" Amanda said. "Send them all your biggest love. Come on! You can do it!"

Come on! Winnie thought toward her seeds. *I love you! You can do it! Grow!*

"And … time." Amanda stood at the front of the

room looking down the row at her volunteers. Whereas a moment ago everyone had seemed relaxed and thoroughly enjoying themselves, now Winnie could see the tension among everyone in the room.

Did any of this work?

"Okay, we're going to open our hands, all at the same time," Amanda said. "Ready … set … show!"

Silence for a few seconds, then a collective *Ohhhhh...*

Then exclamations of surprise. More laughter. And everyone got up to look at everyone else's.

Max had the most seeds sprout. It was incredible. Whereas most of Winnie's seeds now showed white tips on both ends, and a few of them even had short little white tendrils just beginning to show, Max's seeds, almost to a one, had all sprouted little hairs that were at least an inch long, maybe longer, and all twining together like climbing vines.

It looked like his own seedling hair band.

"Wow," Amanda said, looking at his outstretched palm. She took pictures. Her lab assistants were filming all of it.

Others took pictures, too: of their own seeds and of Max's. His wheat berries were the undisputed stars.

For the first time, Winnie thought to look at his twin sister's. Irina had cupped them between her hands again, protectively, as if they might get too cold outside their cocoon.

Winnie lifted her eyebrow. Irina shrugged. She lifted her top hand and showed the seeds only to Winnie.

Irina leaned close and whispered, "Overachiever."

The seeds in Irina's hands had grown twice as much as her brother's. The thin wispy tendrils made a nest of soft curly white that covered Irina's palm.

She couldn't keep the secret for long. Amanda looked over Winnie's shoulder and gave a loud, impressed whistle.

"Sorry, Max," Amanda said, "your sister wins again."

Soon everyone came crowding around. Spontaneous applause broke out. And more laughter. Irina was obviously pleased, but also not grandstanding about it. She gave a little bow, but she seemed as delighted and amazed as any of them.

And her little brother by two minutes bowed back to her. Winnie watched his face. He did not seem the least bit jealous. Instead, he smiled with pride at what his sister had done.

Winnie loved to see it. Not every sibling relationship was so supportive.

Her brother Steven used to tease her mercilessly when it was just between the two of them, but if any outsiders dared criticize or ridicule or bully his little sister, the hackles came up and he was always Winnie's staunchest defender.

"All right!" Amanda said, clapping her hands for

attention. "Please put your babies back to bed in their paper towels and my assistants will come around and take measurements. Please keep your headbands on. We'll move on to the next experiment in just a few minutes. Unless you need to take a break."

Irina sighed. "And now I need to go again." Winnie helped her carefully remove the headband of wires, then Irina headed for the door.

One of the other volunteers, a short, round, balding man who looked several years older than Winnie—*seventy-seven*, she heard in her head—caught Winnie's eye and smiled and gave her a nod. He was clean-shaven with a jowly face and heavy bags under his eyes. His smile was nice and wide. He looked like a friendly Basset Hound.

There was no mistaking his life as an old academic. Even from a distance, Winnie would have been able to pick him out. The worn, dark brown corduroy trousers, threadbare in places and slightly frayed at the hems; the faded brown checkered shirt, open enough at the collar to show a grayish-white T-shirt underneath; a stretched out old brown knit vest that buttoned up the front. Everything looked at least thirty years old, except his shoes, which were a surprise: a pair of sturdy low hikers in the same brand Winnie liked to wear.

Here was a man dressed for comfort, not fashion. His clothes were old, but clean. Some people might think he looked shabby. But Winnie had known enough retired professors over the years to appreciate their relaxed style. She took advantage of it herself, wearing what felt good, what she could breathe in, in colors that made her feel cheerful, without worrying whether her outfits met anyone else's measure of taste.

And of course the man's entire ensemble had been taken up a notch by the long wire wig trailing from his bald head down the back of his neck.

Winnie smiled back at him. Apparently that was enough to break the ice.

"Impressive," said the man, motioning with his chin toward Irina's seeds. "I think only two of mine sprouted." He smiled bashfully. "They must know I have a black thumb."

Winnie wanted to keep the man talking. He had the most delightful accent. Not that high British aristocracy sound, but more like one of the farmers from that show in the Yorkshire Dales that she loved so much.

"Are you a professor?" Winnie asked, already knowing he was. It wasn't just his outfit. An image flashed into her mind of the man lecturing to a full auditorium of students.

"Plant physiology," the man said. He held up his palms in surrender. "I know. I appreciate the irony. My mum was a gard'ner, and I keep thinking some of that *must* have come down to me, but so far … I love a plant, but they don't seem to love me."

Winnie liked his honesty. And his modesty. He was

exactly the kind of character she would enjoy watching in one of her favorite British mystery shows.

"Winnie Parsons," she said, holding out her hand.

"Malcolm Benfry." His hand was dry, a little rough as if he might have just been steering his plow or delivering a calf, and shaking that solid hand gave Winnie a good feeling.

Sometimes just that much contact with a stranger would make Winnie recoil without knowing why. But she trusted her instinct and kept her distance from people like that. Malcolm Benfry seemed like someone she'd like to know.

His name … somehow it tickled the back of Winnie's mind. She had heard it somewhere, or read it, or seen it…

"Five Minute Gardener."

The professor's smile lit up his face. "You know it?"

"*What's all the fuss then?*" Winnie quoted, resisting the urge to do it in a British accent. "*If I can do it, you can do it.*"

"Ah, our celebrity," Irina said, returning to join them. She was taller than Malcolm Benfry by at least four or five inches, and from that height she placed both hands on his shoulders, affectionately, the way a granddaughter might do to a grandfather.

"You should be the one teaching it," Malcolm said, indicating Irina's seeds. Vella the grad student was there at Winnie's and Irina's table now, counting the sprouts and measuring all of the tendrils.

Irina's bounty really was impressive.

"No one wants to hear a Russian tell them to do anything," Irina said. "He has over two hundred thousand subscribers," she told Winnie. "He has fans all over the world."

Professor Benfry waved her away. "They like to see me mess up. Makes them feel good about their own mistakes."

Winnie hadn't thought of it that way, but she realized it was true.

She had watched just a few of his videos over the years, usually when one of her gardening friends sent them to her. She remembered laughing at the one about cutworms. Professor Benfry had some good advice based on his own misadventure of buying a can of cheap coffee and a mini-brewer just so he could generate used coffee grounds to spread under the affected plants.

"Don't do it," he told his viewers. "Stick to tea, for the love of England. I found out something better, and it won't take you five different steps to get there. What's all the fuss? If I can do it, you can do it...."

That was what was so endearing about Malcolm Benfry's videos. He always freely confessed all of his own gardening disasters. Then he'd pick them apart during his short, entertaining videos to share whatever lessons he had to learn the hard way.

Bad soil. Too much sunlight. Not enough sunlight. Seeds too close together or too far apart. Not pruning when he should. Pruning too much. Watering failures. Mulching disasters. Misidentifying the weeds versus the flowers and spending a Saturday pulling up all of the wrong plants. Malcolm Benfry's list of errors went on and on.

And through that, the genial, smiling professor showed the amateur, beginning gardeners that it was all right to make mistakes. He showed it to the experienced gardeners, too. Everyone did it. Everyone messed up at some time. It wasn't a tragedy. Plants died. Plants lived. Keep trying. That's it. You'll learn. *We're all in this togethah...*

"Okay, we're ready for you again," Amanda called out. "Everyone still got their wires on?"

Winnie helped Irina place hers back in position at an angle across her skull. They clipped the receiver unit back onto the waistband of her pants. Winnie noticed Professor Benfry's was in one of the pockets at the front of his vest.

It reminded Winnie of the old days of wearing a lavaliere microphone during a lecture. She always had to be conscious of not disconnecting its cord by catching it on something or accidentally snagging it with her hand.

Plenty of researchers had switched to wireless equipment by now, but Winnie was used to the way Amanda Birkauer did things. The mind lab still used connected sensors in experiments. Amanda felt she got better instrument readings that way.

"We're going to start sending you into the Vault," Amanda told everyone. "Two pairs at a time. Who wants to go first?"

With a grin at Winnie, Irina immediately raised her hand.

"Come on," Irina whispered to Malcolm Benfry. "Get it over with!"

He, too, raised his rough, arthritic-looking hand. Winnie saw Malcolm's partner, a tall thin man with a questionable goatee, scowl.

Too bad, Winnie thought. You're here to try things. Why else would you volunteer at the lab?

"Great," Amanda said. She pointed to two opposite corners at the rear of the room. Winnie knew these booths. She had been in one before. Exciting things usually happened in what Amanda called the Vault.

The booths were copper-lined and sound proof. Stepping into them, the air suddenly felt dead and silent. And normally, Amanda would either dim the lights in there or even turn them out entirely.

The mind did strange things, Winnie had found, when sensory stimulation was taken away. Her first time in the booth, years ago, she learned new pathways into her clairvoyance that she doubted she would ever have found otherwise.

Vella led Winnie and Irina to the booth toward the rear left of the room. Inside, two swivel chairs had been set up choo-choo train style, one in front of the other.

"You can sit in front," Vella told Irina. "Professor Parsons, you're in back."

She put Winnie behind Irina, with her back toward the door.

Once they took their seats, Vella checked their wires to make sure everything was still transmitting.

Winnie knew that just a few steps away, regular life on earth still existed. But here, inside the booth, she felt like she was on a spaceship. She wouldn't have been surprised to feel herself floating upward, untethered by gravity. The sensation inside the Vault was surreal. The sound was unlike anywhere else.

"Testing," Vella said. "Please repeat that."

"Testing," Irina said.

"Testing," Winnie answered.

The words fell into dead space. And yet they had a strange, momentary echo to them, as if their voices were tuning forks that struck the sides of the walls, then were quickly stifled.

Irina swiveled around in her chair and smiled at Winnie. "How straaaange…" She drew out the word, as if testing to hear how strange it really was.

Winnie was tempted to run her index finger up and down on her lips to make a burbling noise. She had done that before when Amanda showed her, and the sound and sensation made Winnie feel like she was sitting somewhere underwater.

But before Winnie could resort to any hijinks, Amanda Birkauer herself appeared at the entrance to the Vault.

"Right," Amanda said quietly. Or maybe she was speaking normally, and the interior of the booth stole any volume. "This experiment is about sending healing energy to the person in front of you. It doesn't even have to be healing. Just think about sending as much life force as you can. It's just ten minutes. Do your best. Please don't speak to each other or say anything out loud. We'll flick the lights when it's time, then the two of you rotate your chairs around, so then Irina, you're sending to Winnie. Got it?"

Winnie and Irina both answered yes, but their words fell flat on the dead air.

Amanda gave Winnie's shoulder a squeeze, then she quietly closed the door to the booth. Soon the lights began to dim. They flickered once, and then Winnie and Irina were plunged into darkness.

Winnie's heart sped up. Without any visual grounding, and in the deadened air of the booth, she could have been floating in outer space for all she knew. She had felt this sensation before, but it still grabbed her every time at the beginning of a Vault experiment, and she had to remind herself to breathe.

She could hear Irina breathing, too, maybe a little harder than normal, although it was difficult to tell in this environment.

Sending life force. Send healing energy...

And then Winnie's mind went someplace else.

And handed her a puzzle she didn't expect.

7

Irina, the younger Irina Winnie had watched her twin brother cry over in the hospital, sat in a pool of light.

At the outer edges it had a yellow cast to it, almost golden, but there was also a whiteness to it in the center, so white it felt pure. So white the pool of light felt solid, like a platform made of marble.

Irina knelt on it, confined to it like someone drifting on a slab of ice in the middle of a frozen ocean.

"Irina?" Winnie said.

Irina answered something in Russian. Her forehead wrinkled as she spoke. She seemed confused. Or distressed. Winnie couldn't tell.

Irina wore a hospital gown that drooped from her shoulders. She seemed thin. Slight. Maybe even emaciated. Winnie couldn't tell. The fabric draped loosely and puddled around Irina's knees.

Winnie remembered Amanda's instruction. No matter how distracting this image of younger Irina was, Winnie concentrated and began to send her healing energy. Life force. That was the assignment.

I send you love ... I send you healing ... I send you energy ... I send you love...

Irina raised her chin and looked at Winnie. Winnie could see the distress, the fear in Irina's dark eyes. Irina's hospital gown shook as her body shivered.

"Are you here ... for me?" Irina asked softly.

"Yes," Winnie said in her mind. Although she wondered if she might have said it out loud. Because it felt like Irina's question had come through Winnie's ears. Had somehow penetrated the dead air of the booth to reach Winnie's hearing.

Winnie stood just steps away from where Irina knelt floating on her slab of white light. So close she wanted to go to her, to gather the thin young woman in her arms and hold her and protect her.

I send you love ... I send you healing...

Irina continued gazing into Winnie's eyes. She seemed so weak, so sad, not at all the luminous, joyful woman Winnie had met today. What happened to her? She was obviously sick. With what? What was going on?

The lights in the booth flickered.

Somehow, impossibly, ten minutes had already gone by.

Winnie wasn't ready to stop. She couldn't. Irina looked at her desperately. This wasn't some experiment anymore, it felt too real. Winnie and Irina had stepped outside normal time and were sharing this isolated experience together.

Part of Winnie's mind, the logical part, knew they were still sitting in the Vault, and even if it wasn't pitch black, all she would be able to see of Irina was the back of her head and the back of her chair.

She also recalled, vaguely, that they were supposed to swivel around now and both face the other direction.

Winnie wasn't about to do that. She didn't want to disturb a single thing about what was happening.

The lights had come on briefly with a soft glow, but Winnie blocked them out with her mind.

She concentrated on Irina, on the young woman in the hospital gown gazing helplessly at Winnie with her dark eyes.

"I'm sending you love, Irina," Winnie told her. "I'm sending you healing. You survive this. I've met you. You're older. You survived. You're so happy. You're perfectly well. Strong and healthy. I've seen you."

Irina stared at Winnie in disbelief.

Tears slid down Irina's cheeks.

It was too much for Winnie to bear. She couldn't

just stand here, keeping her distance, when the poor young woman needed comforting and reassurance.

There was water between them. Cold, freezing water. Too wide for Winnie to jump across. Too deep for her to wade through.

Winnie closed her eyes. Pleaded. *Let me help her. Help me get to her...*

Irina reached out a thin arm toward Winnie and somehow that was enough to bring her over. As if that was what was needed. It wasn't enough that Winnie wanted to help her, Irina had to want that, too.

"Poor girl." Winnie knelt next to Irina and gathered the shivering young woman in her arms. The way Winnie had hugged other people's children over the years. Providing love and support and safety.

Irina began to sob. Winnie could feel her ribs under her hands on Irina's back as the young woman gulped in air and heaved it back out. This was more than simple crying. It felt like Irina was releasing the pent up fears of a lifetime. The collected pain of years.

Winnie gently patted her back. "It's all right ... it's all right..."

"I live?" Irina asked against the fabric of Winnie's shirt. It was then that Winnie saw herself, saw the white coat and the blue scrubs underneath it. She was dressed as a doctor or a nurse. Strange. But this whole vision, if that is what it was, was strange. Winnie could only keep playing her part.

"You live," Winnie told her. "I promise. I've already met you five years later." The years were a guess, but Winnie thought she was close enough.

Four years ten months, her mind told her. It had been a good guess.

Irina let out one last great sob, then pulled back from Winnie and looked up into her face. Tears still wet Irina's cheeks, but Winnie thought she saw a little color there, too. A little more life.

"I don't die," Irina said in her distinctive Russian accent.

"You don't die," Winnie confirmed. "You're one of the happiest people I've ever met. You're more full of life than you can imagine."

That seemed to satisfy younger Irina. She let out a weary sigh.

"Thank you, Doctor." Then she thanked her again in Russian, a word Winnie had heard in movies and on TV. It sounded like *spaseebuh.*

And to her surprise, Winnie answered with some Russian phrase she knew she didn't know. But it made Irina smile.

And then the lights in the booth flickered again. Then slowly they came up. Irina still sat in her chair in front of Winnie, but she had swiveled around at some point and was facing Winnie now.

And she and Irina were holding each other's hands.

They both locked eyes, surprised.

Winnie was about to say something, ask her how she was, but the door to the booth opened behind her, and Vella stuck her head inside.

And like two guilty pupils who had disobeyed their teacher's instructions, they abruptly released each other's hands and leaned backward into their chairs.

If Vella noticed, she didn't say anything. "Please don't talk," she told them. "We'll interview you separately. You can take your headpieces off, though. We're taking a break now."

Irina stretched out her arms as if she had just woken from a satisfying nap. She smiled at Winnie. A friendly, normal smile. Not the smile of someone who had gone through what Winnie just witnessed.

But then, as Vella helped first Winnie and then Irina take off their wire wigs, Winnie thought she saw something in Irina's expression when she caught Winnie glancing at her.

Something … uncomfortable. Uneasy.

As if maybe she did know something of what had just gone on with Winnie.

But then the moment passed, and Irina handed the collection of wires to Vella, and she scooted past Winnie out of the booth, no doubt in a hurry to get to the restrooms.

Winnie still felt rattled by everything she had seen. She felt … incomplete. As if she were still in the middle of watching a drama and suddenly the power had gone out and she didn't know how it ended.

Amanda was waiting outside the booth. She glanced at Winnie, then seeing whatever she saw, she looked at her harder.

"Okay?" Amanda asked.

"Not sure," Winnie answered.

Amanda smiled. "Well, this should be interesting."

8

It took a few minutes before the next two pairs of volunteers were settled inside the Vaults. Winnie waited as patiently as she could, going over everything she saw, felt, and heard so she could report it all to Amanda.

But she also went over it for herself. What, exactly, was that?

Was it a vision? Winnie knew what that was like. This felt close to one … but not quite.

Was it what Amanda Birkauer told them it would be, just a healing experiment inside the copper-lined, sound-proofed booth, and it was because of the booth that Winnie's mind had gone further, maybe, than it otherwise would?

But what was that? Winnie continued to wonder. It felt real. It felt true.

Not an experiment, but an experience. One Winnie had physically and mentally participated in, even though Irina didn't seem especially affected by it.

Vella was off with Irina at one of the tables now, interviewing her about what she experienced. Winnie hoped Amanda would share that with her later. She needed to know if Irina saw anything like what Winnie did.

Finally Amanda was free. She motioned for Winnie to come to one of the individual Scandinavian tables off in the corner of the room, far from the rest of the group. Those who were waiting for their turns in the booths took advantage of their free time by reading their phones, chatting with each other, or milling around in the hallway to have some solitary time to themselves.

That would have been Winnie's choice. But what she wanted right now was to talk to her friend about what on earth had just gone on.

Winnie described it all. In as much detail as she could. Amanda asked a few follow-up questions for clarification, but mostly she took rapid-fire notes in penmanship so awful even Amanda admitted she sometimes couldn't read her own writing.

More than once she'd shown something she wrote to Winnie, to look at it with fresh eyes.

"Can you tell what that says?" Amanda would ask her.

Winnie would look at it, not too closely, but with a softened gaze. Trying to take in the scrawls as a whole.

And more times than not, Winnie could decipher it. Whether it was through her clairvoyance or just being used to Amanda's hieroglyphics, it was hard to tell.

Winnie half-wished Amanda would slow down now, make sure the notes were clear, but she also half-wished Amanda was writing exactly as fast as she was, to get this all down while the details were still fresh in Winnie's mind.

"So she didn't recognize you," Amanda said. "Not from meeting you today."

"No," Winnie said. "She definitely thought I was someone else. A doctor."

"Well..." Amanda paused and tapped her pen against her notebook.

Winnie knew that look. "What?"

Amanda hesitated, then said it. "I was going to tell you this afterward. I know you don't like to be influenced."

That was true. Generally Winnie liked to come in to Amanda's experiments without any bias. She wanted to keep her own reactions clean.

But Winnie didn't want to be kept in the dark this time. The experience had been too strange. If Amanda had some insight, Winnie needed to know.

"I was going to assign you to a different partner today," Amanda said. "One of the Brits. I knew you'd want that."

"Of course," Winnie said. Amanda understood her perfectly.

"But I was talking to Irina when you walked into the lab this morning, and I swear, she just lit up. *Oh! Who is that?* I told her you were my friend Dr. Parsons. She said, *Doctor?* And I said PhD in Psychology. She … I don't know," Amanda said. "Was she a little disappointed?"

"That I wasn't a medical doctor?" Winnie asked.

"Maybe," Amanda said. "Or maybe I'm just projecting now, because of what you told me."

The two of them paused to consider that. Amanda wanted true, clean experiments, too.

"In any case," Amanda said, "she was very enthusiastic about being paired with you. She specifically asked if she could. So I went with it. Why not."

"Do you think she … recognized me?" Winnie asked.

"I have no idea." Amanda shook her head. "Now this all feels like too much speculation. Let's just go back to what we know."

Amanda asked her more questions about how Irina seemed after the lights came up. Yes, they were holding hands, which was unexpected—Winnie couldn't remember when that might have happened, unless it was when the Irina in her vision reached out her hand and Winnie took it.

But when the lights came up Winnie couldn't say there had been any meaningful eye contact, no knowing nod from Irina, nothing to indicate that she was conscious of the conversation she had just had with Winnie.

Except that one fleeting moment when Winnie thought she saw a change to Irina's expression. But it was there and gone so quickly, Winnie couldn't truthfully interpret it.

"Let's go back to what I said to Irina," Winnie said. "Here I am now, today, talking to her in the past—almost five years ago—about meeting her here today and knowing she survived."

Winnie paused to make sure she had said it in the accurate order.

Amanda understood her perfectly. And she understood the significance. "Yeah, what about that."

"Have you ever heard of some kind of time..." Winnie wasn't certain how to describe it. "I don't know, time going back and forth like that?"

"Sure," Amanda said. "Have a beer with a physicist and it's all they want to talk about. Time loops and influencing the past from the present, and the future reaching back to influence us now ... at least I'll have something to add next time I'm stuck with one at a conference."

Winnie closed her eyes. Tried to process what Amanda just said.

Behind her she could hear Vella and Geoffrey herding the last sets of volunteers into the two booths.

Winnie opened her eyes and watched Amanda scribble another several paragraphs of illegible notes.

Winnie waited for a pause.

When she had Amanda's full attention again, she asked the question that was foremost in her mind.

"Do you think that was real?"

Amanda knew what she was asking. And Winnie knew she took the question seriously. Amanda thought about it before answering.

"Let's say, for the sake of argument," Amanda said, "that my physicist friends are right, and time is a malleable loop. Not just one and done, straight forward, the past is the past and there's nothing we can do about it."

Winnie nodded. She was with her so far.

"You have already proven many times," Amanda said, "that the future can be seen and changed. That it isn't written in stone."

"Right." And it was true. Winnie had seen things—like the bridge being out on a rainy, remote country road, had seen her family's car take the curve too fast and not be able to stop in time, and plunge into the river, drowning all of them.

But she altered that future by shouting out to her father to hit the brakes.

Which he did, although that was a moment of choice. He could have chosen to ignore his 12-year-old daughter and live—and die—in the future she saw.

Amanda pinched her fingers against her eyes. "And then this is where it gets tricky. Which future? Which present? What if you or Irina hadn't come to do the experiments today? What if you never met? What if I didn't put you in the Vault and tell you to send healing energy?" Amanda smiled. "It's fascinating and it's maddening, and that's what gets me up in the morning. So your guess is as good as mine. Let's just see where all this goes."

She stood up, as if that was as far as they could take it at the moment.

But Winnie was already taking it further.

She was thinking of something else. Someone else. On another day, in another room, here in the Psychology basement to participate in another experiment.

What if he hadn't? What if she hadn't? What if this or that had been different in any number of details?

And what about what Amanda described, of Irina seeing Winnie—this present Winnie she had never met before—and acting so excited to see her? Asking to be paired with her? Why? What did she sense—or remember?

Remember of what hadn't happened yet?

Or had it already happened, five years ago, when Irina was sick in the hospital?

Tricky didn't begin to describe it.

But now that it was in Winnie's mind, she couldn't dismiss it.

Had she and Joe already met, sometime, somewhere? In a different time, maybe the future?

Is that why he seemed so familiar to her? Is that why he instantly felt what he told her he felt?

And if Winnie hadn't come to this experiment today, would she ever even know enough to ask these questions?

Sometimes all she could tell herself was that the Magic of Timing was real. People showed up when they needed to. Events happened exactly when they should.

Wasn't that how people used to explain strange phenomena before anyone had heard of modern science?

It's magic.

Winnie didn't exactly believe in magic—or even know exactly what it was—but some things just defied normal explanation. Just as many people didn't believe in the paranormal, when Winnie and Amanda and anyone else paying attention knew it was absolutely real.

Winnie saw Vella and Geoffrey both flicker the light

switches on their respective booths, signaling the second half of those experiments. Winnie had ten more minutes to go clear her mind. Relax and let information come to her again, and not keep trying so hard to figure it all out.

On her way out of the room to visit the restroom and just be by herself, Irina intersected her at the door. She looked confused. Maybe even a little distressed.

"I think I need to apologize," Irina told her.

"For what?"

"For what I said to you in the Vault."

Winnie's heart beat a little faster. So Irina did remember after all.

"What did you say?" Winnie asked, ready for confirmation.

Irina tilted her head. Gave Winnie a funny look. As if anyone would remember.

"About being lonely," Irina said. "That wasn't kind of me."

Now it was Winnie's turn to look confused. "What did you say? When?"

"About your husband. Joe. About the plane crash. I shouldn't have—"

Winnie clutched her arm. "Irina, you never said a thing about him. We only talked about you. You were sick and I told you everything was going to be..."

But Winnie could see from her face that Irina didn't

remember any of that. She was just as confused as Winnie.

"Hold on," Winnie said. Despite her mind wanting her to stay and hash this out, her bladder was ready to burst. "I'll be right back. Then we need to talk to Amanda."

9

As soon as Winnie returned from a rapid trip to the restroom, she headed straight for Amanda Birkauer, motioning for Irina to come, too.

The two of them had to wait at the periphery while Amanda gave instructions to her two lab assistants.

"What's up?" Amanda asked once Vella and Geoffrey went off to their tasks.

"I wanted you here when Irina told me," Winnie said. "I think this is going to be significant."

Amanda looked from Winnie to Irina. "Look, I'm sorry. I really want to," she said. "But this is my last day with everyone, and I still need to get to three more experiments. Can it wait?"

Winnie felt like a three-year-old, hopping from one foot the other, feeling like she was going to burst with some news. *I saw a lion! I lost a tooth!* But in Winnie's case, *Irina saw something completely different than I did! And she knows something about Joe!*

But Winnie could empathize with her friend. She knew what it was like to have a jam-packed agenda, to want to get everything accomplished on a set and tight schedule without anyone throwing in a wrench.

So Winnie had to calm her racing heart. "Sure," she said, trying hard to mean it, even though at the moment that was impossible. "We can wait."

Irina broke in. "I'm sorry, but I really don't know what this is about."

Winnie nodded. "I know. It can wait. I'm sure you'll remember everything."

She hoped it was true. She had to believe it was true. Just as Winnie knew in her heart she would remember every detail of her healing session with Irina, whether she talked about it now or in five hours from now.

She only hoped she didn't have to wait that long.

Amanda had told her when she invited Winnie to the lab that it would probably end by 4:30. It mattered because Winnie didn't like to leave Clover and Arthur alone past dinner. That wasn't fair to the dogs. Dinner delayed was dinner denied, especially as far as a Labrador was concerned, and besides, Winnie and the dogs kept each other company. It wasn't fun to be left alone all day.

Winnie looked at the clock. It was a little after 11:00. They would probably break for lunch at some point, probably after one more experiment. Then two more experiments in the afternoon. It all made sense, and normally Winnie wouldn't even bother looking at the clock. She'd just show up and enjoy whatever came.

And she knew she could ask Irina to tell her privately, right now, to spit it out and not have to wait another second.

But Winnie wanted Amanda to hear it, too. Her friend was a brilliant scientist and researcher and always had insights Winnie valued. Many times Amanda saw things in Winnie's clairvoyance that Winnie was so used to herself, it didn't even register anymore. Like her ability to read people's moods at a distance, just by tuning in to some subtle vibration from the energy field around them. It was second nature to Winnie, a skill she could turn on and off, and it was a way she learned to protect herself when she was young from kids in school who might seem outwardly nice, but were really sour and mean underneath.

So now, if the choice was between hearing Irina tell the story to just Winnie, or to Winnie and Amanda together, Winnie knew it was better that they hear it together. And not only because of Amanda's insights.

Irina had already told the story of their healing session once, to the lab assistant Vella. Winnie saw that debriefing while she gave hers to Amanda. Winnie had no idea what Irina said, but she did know that the more times Irina told the same story, the less pure the information would be over time. Not on purpose, but just because that was how the human mind worked.

A whole body of psychological studies described the unconscious human tendency to embellish a story the more times the person told it. In came up all the time in criminal law. It was why an eyewitness's first statement about what had happened was usually more reliable than the second or third or fourth time they told it.

People might not want to embellish it or edit, but they couldn't help themselves. They would have already heard themselves tell the story once, and then their brains naturally took over and began analyzing, second-guessing, and tweaking.

Winnie could tell that Irina was the type of person who would try very hard to get it right. And so was it really such a risk to ask her to tell the story now, privately to Winnie, and then tell it again to Amanda later to bring in her always-insightful analysis?

But Winnie knew that if she could just be wise and patient and wait, she might be rewarded with a more accurate story.

Even though the suspense might very well drive her out of her mind.

So she would wait. Wait for this afternoon, wait for

Amanda, wait—although she could hardly believe it when she heard Irina say his name—for Joe.

The plane crash.

How did Irina know? *What* did she know?

"Is everything all right?" Irina asked Winnie, no doubt seeing the tension on her face.

Winnie forced herself to relax. Forced herself to smile. She needed to slow her heart down and keep her mind from racing ahead.

"Everything is fine," Winnie said. She gave Irina's arm a light squeeze. "We'll talk later. When we have plenty of time."

Irina searched Winnie's face one more time with her inquisitive black eyes, then gave her a nod and went off to talk to her brother.

While Winnie stood alone and allowed her emotions to finish swirling around and find a way to settle.

The truth was, even though three years had gone by since Joe last breathed here on earth, Winnie still looked for him, thought of him, still dreamed of him.

She had no illusions. She knew he was gone. But she also knew that the human spirit was more than just wispy vapors on a movie screen. The afterlife might not be what screenwriters made it look like, but Winnie knew there was a reality behind stories of life after death.

And she knew enough about Joe's own brush with

death after his plane broke apart over the ocean to know that there was more to human existence than what society was willing to admit. Joe had seen things when Winnie hypnotized him to help him unlock his buried memories.

Winnie had listened. She believed him. And it helped her to know after he died that his death—this second death—was still not the end.

Even though she longed to feel the touch of Joe's hand on hers. To feel his arms around her again. To hear his voice and the things he said.

I'm sorry I said you were lonely, Irina had said.

Why apologize? Irina was right. Winnie was lonely. Not in the abstract—she had plenty of friends, she had family, she had Clover and little Arthur. But for all of her rebuilding to make a life on her own now, of course she still felt the pangs of loneliness. Joe was the love of her life. She wasn't crying and grieving for him every day anymore, but she still missed him. How could she not?

So if Irina had seen something … if she knew something … Winnie just had to know.

But there was nothing for it. For now, Winnie had to wait.

10

"All right, everybody," Amanda commanded the group, "let's get your headsets back on. Time to find out what other powers you have."

Near the front of the room the two lab assistants had moved some of the tables out of the way to set up two different tables that brought smiles of recognition to the faces of some of the participants.

Winnie had no idea what they were supposed to be.

They were two long folding tables with metal bases and white plastic tops, just like the kind she had at home. She'd bring it out and set it up if she had a sewing project she wanted to do, or if more people were coming over for dinner than she could comfortably fit at her regular kitchen table.

The two folding tables were covered in the standard

navy blue nylon tablecloths Winnie had seen the U of A use for most campus events the past few years, stretched taut across the tables and anchored at their feet.

But beyond that, Amanda and her two assistants had made some curious modifications.

They must have used box cutters to take apart some large packing boxes. Then they taped the cardboard panels and braced them around all four sides of the tables. They made high sides on the lengths and the back of the tables, leaving a shorter strip of cardboard at what Winnie thought of as the two fronts.

It was an impressive craft project. But Winnie still had no clue what it was about.

"In case you haven't figured it out yet," Amanda told the participants, "today is about testing mind over matter. Or energy over matter—I'll let you decide which you think it is."

She held up two small cellophane packages in her left palm and crinkled them for effect.

"What are we doing?" Amanda asked the crowd.

A British voice answered, "We're playing craps."

"That's right," Amanda said, smiling. She pointed to the man who gave the right answer. It was Professor Benfry of the gardening mishaps.

Amanda handed him one of the unopened packages and kept the other for herself.

"Who here has been to Vegas?" Amanda asked.

Several of the Brits raised their hands. Winnie did not. She'd never had a reason to go there, and so never had. The Russian twins left their hands down, too.

But there was no mistaking the excitement on Irina's face. She caught Winnie looking, and grinned.

"Here is your assignment," Amanda said. "We'll do two rounds, ten throws each. We know, statistically, how many doubles should show up. So that's your job: roll as many doubles as you can. Try to beat the statistics. You can talk to the dice, sing to them, send them energy—however you want to do it. But the goal is to make them fall the way you want. Got it?"

There was a murmur of laughter among the group. Winnie smiled. Amanda loved to come up with games to test psychic ability. She said it kept people from getting bored in the lab. Even the extraordinary could start to feel too ordinary after a while. That was why she kept her experiments short in duration, and liked to move from one to another before the volunteers started to feel stale.

Winnie had never seen Amanda use this particular game. She was anxious to try it for herself.

The group divided themselves without discussion into two separate teams. Winnie saw Amanda point that out to Vella, who pulled out a notebook and began writing down the names.

"Oh, and one more thing," Amanda said. She gestured to the crowd. "You all have a part to play, too.

You've probably read about the home team advantage. How local fans can actually change the dynamics of a game. So we're testing all of you, even when someone else is rolling the dice. Send as much energy as you can. It might help. Okay, ready, everybody? Let's GO!"

Amanda set the tone by clapping her hands hard, fan-style, and whooping to the first two people who stepped in front of the mock craps tables. One was Professor Malcolm Benfry, the other was a tall, slender, severe-looking British man wearing a tweed suit complete with vest and jacket and bow tie.

But as Amanda kept cheering and clapping, Winnie saw the tall Brit smile. And soon others around the tables were joining in the clapping and shouting. It was infectious. Winnie added her voice and hands to the cheering and clapping and found herself laughing just as others were. Because it was silly, but also fun.

The two British men opened up their cellphone packages and removed their respective pairs of dice. Then they both glanced at each other at the same time, in what must have felt like an irresistible moment of rivalry.

"Come on, snake eyes!" Amanda shouted. "Come on, sixes! Whoo! Let's do it! Come on!"

"Come on, BENFRY!" Irina shouted, grinning and cheering. She stood beside Winnie, thunderously clapping her hands. Her joyful smile lifted Winnie's heart. To have seen the young woman looking so sick, so sad

—and now this. It was hard to picture the other Irina now, when this healthy, vibrant one continued shouting out encouragement to her British professor friend with the enthusiasm of a fan at a hockey game.

Across from Winnie and Irina on the other side of their table stood a dowdy-looking British woman in a woolen skirt, pale pink sweater set, and sensible shoes. But even she shouted out a lusty, "COME ON, DOUBLES!" as the two men launched their first throws.

The crowd erupted in cheers. Double fours for Professor Benfry, a five and a six for the other Brit.

"Close!" Amanda shouted to the tall thin man. "You can do it! Come on, Michael!"

And while the crowd cheered and clapped and hurrayed, the men kept throwing doubles and near-doubles almost every time.

When their ten tries were up, everyone seemed relieved to be able to stop. It was exhausting being so happy. That's what it was, Winnie realized. Everyone was happy.

"Outstanding!" Amanda told the first two rollers. "Who's next? Let's keep it going!"

Everyone rallied and cheered and encouraged the players on. Roll after roll, doubles kept coming up. Winnie knew they must already be beating the statistics. Irina's twin rolled eight out of ten doubles, the highest of any of them. Max raised his arms in triumph at the end, and he hopped up and down like a boxer who had just won a prize fight.

He pointed at his older sister by two minutes, and Irina gave a shrug as she laughed and continued cheering. She had only managed seven out of ten doubles—the record until Max took his turn. The twins were even now, one win to one, with Irina's wheat berry sprouting performance outstripping his.

Winnie wondered what Amanda's remaining two experiments would be. And which twin would come out on top at the end.

But she couldn't go any further with her speculation, because though Winnie had been delaying her turn until everyone else in her group went, finally the time was here.

She knew she should have felt tired from all her nonstop clapping and shouting and laughing, but instead she felt electric. Ready. Pumped. Alive.

Winnie's first throw came up double twos. Everyone cheered. Then she threw a one and a four and they groaned. At the other table a stocky British man with a walrus mustache alternated his rolls with Winnie's so they could each see how the other one did.

Winnie took a deep breath. This was roll number three. She wanted to concentrate, to really try.

She cupped the dice between her hands and murmured encouragement to them, *You can do it!* Then she launched them down the table and waited while they bounced and rolled.

A one and a four. Again.

Winnie reset, murmured to her dice, threw.

A one and a four again.

She looked at Amanda, who raised an eyebrow. There had to be some statistics saying what Winnie was doing was out of the ordinary, but the assignment was to roll doubles, and Winnie wasn't giving up.

She cupped the dice again and changed her pep talk. *You're fantastic. You're the best. I love you. You're my favorites...*

Double threes.

"Well done!" shouted the man with the walrus mustache. He threw again and got double sixes.

The two tables were hot.

Winnie had five throws left.

She tried to put herself in the Zone, whatever that might be. But she thought she could feel it, a kind of electric buzz, but also a floaty feeling, as if everything were moving in slow motion and if Winnie kept her energy at a certain frequency, she could almost imagine the mystical connection with her dice.

Throw numbers six, seven, and eight: Double fours, every one of them.

The crowd went wild. The walrus mustache Brit reached over and gave her a gentle pat on the back. He had managed a few more doubles himself. The two of them were the highest scoring pair.

And then Winnie felt her concentration start to wobble. She couldn't sustain it anymore. Her last two throws came up the same they had before: a one and a four, twice.

Again Amanda gave her a quizzical look. Winnie knew it was probably strange to have rolled that non-double combination so many times, but she had no idea what it meant. That was for Amanda Birkauer and her research team to figure out.

The walrus man ended with one last double, bringing his total to six out of ten.

"Max is our winner!" Amanda shouted to the group. "Runner up, Irina!"

The twins gave cheerful, modest little bows, first to the group, and then to each other.

Once again Winnie enjoyed that feeling of watching two siblings who really liked each other.

"All right!" Amanda shouted. "Let's take a short break! But leave your headsets on. We're not quite done."

But before anyone could leave the room, Amanda added one more wrinkle.

"During break, don't talk to each other. Don't make eye contact. Keep absolutely separate and silent. Got it? Thanks."

Then she turned to her lab assistants and ignored

the participants, who looked at each other for a moment in confusion.

Then Winnie looked away. No eye contact? No talking? It was strange, but if those were the next rules of the next game, she would comply, just like everyone else seemed to be.

All talk abruptly ended. Out of the corner of her eye Winnie could see people walking toward the door with their heads bowed, eyes to themselves.

The walrus mustache man reached the door right ahead of the dowdy British woman in the wool skirt and pink sweater, and Winnie saw him start to say something, *You first*, but then suppress it and just gesture for her to go ahead.

It was an awkward moment, despite the politeness. Because the man looked down at his feet as he did it, not acknowledging the woman with even a glance.

Winnie stood off to the side and watched other people react. As long as she observed at a distance and never made eye contact, she knew she was obeying the rules.

And that was it: They were all, it looked like to Winnie, rule-followers. Not a radical among them. And as a result, the mood of the group felt somber now, all the joy of five minutes ago gone. It was fascinating, how quickly everything had changed. She could feel how charged the air was and how wrong it felt for none of them to be able to celebrate with their comrades the fun they had just had together. Instead it was as if they were all being punished—and for something they didn't do.

Obviously this discomfort Amanda created was part of her next experiment, whatever it was. The headsets with their trails of wires were still recording everyone's brain waves. What did it look like when people wanted to be happy and were told they had to keep it to themselves? What if someone wanted a feeling of community, but was told to stay away, don't even look at anyone else?

Winnie was careful to time her visit to the restroom after Irina had already gone and come back. It would have been too tempting to catch her eye and smile at her. Winnie was a good test subject and tried to give Amanda her best results.

When the break was over and everyone had come back, Amanda gave them their new instructions.

"Ten throws again," she said, her voice quieter now. She was setting the new mood. No clapping and cheering this time. Instead it was as if they were about to tour a library. "Really concentrate," Amanda told them. "Vella and Geoffrey will remind you of your scores when it's your turn. Try to get better by at least one throw. Do your best. Let's begin."

If their mood the first time they played had been a 10, now it felt like a 2. All the air had gone out of the fun. Professor Benfry and Michael the tall thin Brit stepped up and took their places as the first throwers. They both seemed to be concentrating hard. One threw, and then the other. Both threw double fives.

"Shhh," Amanda warned everyone, holding her finger to her lips. "No cheering. Again," she told the two men quietly.

And then nothing seemed to work for them.

Not a single double between them. Even though before each throw, the men paused, thought, concentrated.

"Very good," Amanda said flatly when their ten tries were over. "Who's next?"

It felt like a very long school lesson. Like factory work. Just throw, get the dice back, concentrate, throw.

Winnie looked around at the people surrounding the tables. She caught a few yawns. People were distracted. If they didn't have a part to play, cheering on their friends, what was the point? Was it lunchtime yet? When was this going to be over?

Winnie went last again, and despite the horrible mood of the people around her, she genuinely tried her best to make the dice do what she asked.

Two twos. Two ones. But then that was it for her score. Everything else was a mismatched number—not even her good old one-and-four combo—and then her ten tries were done.

Once Winnie and the man with the walrus

mustache finished their final throws, everyone was quiet for a moment, just waiting.

"Well, that was boring," Amanda said bluntly. "And probably predictable. But we needed to try, just to see."

But then she smiled. With a mischievous lift to one of her eyebrows that Winnie had seen countless times before. Amanda always had something up her sleeve. Of course she wasn't going to let this experiment end on such a depressing note.

"You get two more tries," Amanda said. "Each of you. But here's the catch: It has to be a trick shot."

People looked confused. But a few of them smiled. Irina laughed out loud. She was already getting the picture.

She raised her hand. "This time I will go first."

"Good idea," Amanda said. "Let's break that last cycle." Then she started clapping her hands hard again, the way she did before. "All right, Irina! Come on! Show us what you GOT!"

Winnie could sense the hesitation in the crowd. As if they were afraid to fall for it. As if Amanda had already broken their trust.

"Come on!" Amanda cheered, pumping her arms and trying to lift the mood. "Let's go! This is the fun round! Come on! Just two more rolls! Go, Irina! WOOT!"

That seemed to break the ice. Irina jogged in place, as if warming up, then she cracked her neck side to side and shook out her arms. At last that brought out the smiles again, followed by laughter and cheering and clapping.

"Go, Irina!"

"You can do it!"

"COME ON!" Geoffrey shouted with a voice much louder than Winnie expected from the lab assistant. He rarely spoke up at all.

Irina waved to the crowd as if she were a champion tennis player at Wimbledon. Then she twirled in place like a ballerina, glared at the table with a snarl, and lifted her right thigh and pitched the two dice underneath it.

The dice pitched and bounced and rolled.

Double sixes.

The crowd went wild.

Amanda retrieved the dice and handed them to Irina, who gracefully flapped her arms like a swan, bent at the waist, and launched the dice forward across her back.

Double sixes.

Impossible, and there they were.

Irina beamed. The dowdy British woman hugged her.

And Winnie caught Amanda's eye. Amanda gave her a secret smile.

That, right there, was satisfaction. Amanda had made a plan, without knowing how it would work.

But as the next person stepped up, and then each one after that, taking it in single turns rather than splitting between the two tables so that everyone could cheer together for each individual thrower, Winnie cast a look of admiration at her friend.

The way Amanda Birkauer managed her experiments. It took planning and imagination and guts. These weren't the days anymore of having people go one by one through a deck of Zener cards, testing their ESP. Amanda Birkauer was an original, and Winnie was proud to know her.

When it was his turn, Professor Benfry tucked his arms in his armpits and flapped like a chicken for his first throw and waddled like a penguin for his second. Double twos the first time, a one and a two the second.

"Oh! So close!" Amanda shouted, and the professor seemed happy enough.

When it was Winnie's turn, somewhere in the middle this time instead of deliberately last, she asked the people closest to back away and give her some room. Then she swung her right arm like she'd seen cricket players wind up for a pitch, and after two rotations she turned and threw the dice behind her.

She could tell from the crowd that he hadn't thrown a double.

"What is with you with the one and fours?" Amanda called out.

Winnie wanted to keep up her momentum, so she

hopped twice on one leg and then did Irina's trick of bending over and tossing the dice forward across her back.

Double threes. The crowd cheered and applauded. Winnie stepped aside for dowdy woman and watched her throw doubles on both of her tries. The woman raised both fists in the air and whooped in triumph.

They got through all sixteen people in what felt like a rush of time. Everyone rose to the challenge. Not a single person acted as if a trick shot were beneath them, it wasn't dignified, I'm not playing.

To the contrary, Winnie saw the playfulness erupt from these people who only ten minutes ago had all seemed so depressed and dejected because of Amanda Birkauer's rules.

The power of suggestion. The power of authority. The power of people's energy to affect the falling of a pair of dice.

"You all ready for lunch?" Amanda shouted, and the group shouted back with a united "YES!"

"We have a whole spread next door. Vella will show you over there."

Then as the laughing, happy participants filed out of the room, Amanda plopped into the nearest Scandinavian-looking chair.

Winnie sank into the seat beside her.

"You always have something, don't you?" Winnie said.

Amanda chuckled. "Well, I try. Wait till we see the results of that one. Should be very, very interesting."

Winnie felt tempted to stick around, to take advantage of their friendship by staying in what felt like the teacher's lounge, but she knew from her own years of teaching that even friends could feel like an intrusion. Amanda deserved her own break. And she probably had plenty to do to set up for the next experiments.

"I haven't forgotten," Amanda said. "I know you have something important to tell me. I promise, we'll get to it. As soon as I have the bandwidth."

Winnie didn't feel so impatient and antsy anymore. The last session of cheering her voice hoarse had cured her of that.

She patted Amanda's arm and pushed herself up from her chair.

"It can wait," Winnie said. "But not forever. I think you and Irina need to come over to my house for dinner."

"That good?" Amanda asked. She sat up straight, energized again by even the hint of something mysterious.

"It might be," Winnie told her. "But Clover misses you anyway. And Arthur needs to get to know you. And I think Irina is someone *I'd* like to know."

"Oh, she is," Amanda confirmed. "The stories I could tell you…"

But then Amanda looked at her watch and even

though she might not have meant that as a hint, Winnie took it.

"Want me to bring you some lunch?" she asked Amanda as she headed for the door.

"Vella's making me something," Amanda said. "But thanks. Although I probably won't mind another coffee by the time you come back."

Amanda's internal settings were always set to high, and Winnie knew one way she kept up with herself was by feeding herself often—sometimes two salads a day, on top of energy bars and sandwiches and pasta and plenty of fruit—and by always keeping a fresh pot of coffee at the ready.

Winnie could use a cup of it herself. And some chocolate.

Psychic work always called for more chocolate.

11

Winnie followed the sounds to a room nearby where Vella was just emerging with two paper plates heaped with lunch goodies. Two turkey and cheese sandwiches on what looked like Everything bagels, two bags of barbecue chips, two chocolate and almond energy bars, and two sizable chocolate chip cookies.

Amanda understood how to put on a spread.

"I'll bring her some coffee," Winnie said.

"Oh, thanks," Vella answered with relief. The young woman's hands were already occupied trying to carry everything she had.

"By the way..." Winnie hesitated. Should she? Was this a way to get around the issue of Irina telling her story too many times?

Vella paused and waited. Winnie could see one of the plates begin to tilt. She quickly righted it and rearranged the overloaded bagel sandwich that had been the culprit.

"Are we allowed to know our results?" Winnie asked her. There. The question was out.

"How do you mean?"

"Will we be able to read the notes from our sessions?" Winnie asked.

What she really meant was could she read the notes of what Irina told Vella after their time in the booth.

"I don't know," Vella said. "Sorry. That's up to Dr. Birkauer."

Winnie nodded and let the grad student continue on her way.

She turned back toward the room where lunch was being served and saw Irina standing in the doorway, smiling.

"I'm curious, too," she said. "I want to read everybody's, don't you? All these experiments are so much fun."

"Amanda—Dr. Birkauer…"

Irina waved away the formality. "I know she's your friend. Go on."

"She's always so creative," Winnie said. "I love coming to the lab."

"You're so lucky to have her," Irina said. "I wish we weren't leaving tomorrow, or I'd stay another week."

"Where are you going?"

"Someplace called Sedona," Irina answered. "They say there are energy vortexes there."

Winnie was familiar with the energetic anomalies surrounding Sedona, Arizona.

"Are you on some kind of tour?" she asked Irina.

"A mystical, magical, mystery bus tour," Irina said, laughing. "Some of my old professors and colleagues from Oxford have made ourselves a group. Last year we visited Stonehenge and some of those alien crop circles in England."

"That sounds fun." In fact, it sounded like a lot of fun. Winnie wondered for a moment if they'd let in an outsider.

"I love it," Irina said. "Max isn't even part of our group anymore—he's too busy now—but he always comes along on our trips."

So maybe they would allow an outsider. Winnie tucked that one away.

She followed Irina back into the snack room. Winnie could smell the yeast from freshly-made bagels. All the Everything bagels were already gone, but she found an Asiago cheese and green chili flavor that looked perfect as a sandwich base. She added slices of Havarti cheese—psychic work also seemed to call for a lot of cheese—and slices of tomato and avocado. The bagel felt springy as she cut the sandwich in half. Perfect.

The chips didn't call to her, but the chocolate chip cookies absolutely did. There was a single-serve coffee pot set up, and Winnie made herself a cup of dark roast and added a splash of almond milk. She would bring Amanda her own cup when they were ready to go back to the lab.

The room was too small to provide seating for anyone. The two tables were taken up with food.

Irina helped herself to a second cookie and followed Winnie to a windowless room across the hall that Winnie knew was mostly used for storage, but had a table and a few chairs.

"May I join you ladies?" Professor Benfry asked.

Winnie had just opened the door and peered inside to make sure the table was still in place.

She had hoped to talk to Irina alone, but she still wanted to wait for Amanda before they really dove into the most important topic. So it was easy to be gracious to the British gardening guru.

"Of course," Winnie said with genuine friendliness. "It's a tight squeeze, but I think we can do it."

The table was half the length of the folding tables Amanda had used for her craps experiment. But the three of them found spots around it, the professor pushing aside a stack of banker boxes to free up his chair, and they settled in for their meals.

Professor Benfry had chosen a dark rye bagel that

he spread with mustard and mayonnaise and piled with mostly cheese.

Maybe he knew about the restorative powers of cheese, too.

"So what did you both think?" Malcolm Benfry asked. "About our success at dice?"

"I loved it," Irina answered. "Not the depressing version, but the first and the last."

"The depressing version," Professor Benfry said. "Yes. Most fascinating. It explains a few things I've noticed."

Irina leaned over the table and rested her chin on her hands. "Tell me. You know I love your stories."

Winnie was happy to eat and drink her coffee and listen. She found the British man charming—mostly because he was British, after all—and it was the soundtrack she wanted while she replenished herself with food.

"You know about my pink roses," the professor said.

Irina turned to Winnie. "He planted them for his wife. It's his love garden."

Malcolm Benfry nodded. Winnie caught the tinge of sadness in his eyes. An image came to her mind. Of Professor Benfry crying as he dug his trowel into a patch of dirt. He stopped digging and bent his head and let the tears freely flow. A few of them found their way into the dirt where he knelt.

His love garden. Winnie understood.

"Mavis loved roses," the professor said. "I kept telling her, *I'll plant them, I'll plant them!* But then … time. And one is so busy. Life is so daily, isn't it? And then the next thing you know…"

The professor smiled, softly, not searching for sympathy, Winnie could see, but just for understanding.

Winnie nodded. She did understand.

"So I finally made the time," said Professor Benfry. He paused to take a bite of his cheese and bagel sandwich. He politely covered his mouth while he chewed.

He took a sip from a can of orange-flavored fizzy water, then continued. "I worked on the garden every Saturday for a whole spring and summer. Out there wrestling with the soil, getting poked by rose thorns, watching the petals fall off and the plants die … what was I doing wrong?"

"I have my theory," Irina answered, "but you tell me."

"And what do you say, madam?" Malcolm Benfry asked Winnie. "This one is a genius about soils." He pointed at Irina. "But I think the answer lies elsewhere."

So did Winnie. But she preferred to hear the professor's theory. She could listen to her own voice any time at all. But she only had this one day listening to the British.

And she also wanted to hear how the professor's mind worked. That was more entertaining even than his accent.

So Winnie answered, "You tell me."

"My wife, God bless her, died in the winter six years ago. I cried for seven months straight. November to May. Then I knew I had to get hold of myself. What would Mavis say? But even as I was working in the garden, doing my hardest to make it beautiful, I still thought of her every time and it just wracked me with pain."

Winnie understood more than the professor could know. But this was his story, not hers.

"And then one day, I read something," Malcolm Benfry said. "I don't know if you go in for the philosophers—" He looked from Irina to Winnie, checking for any signs of enthusiasm. Philosophy was fine, but Winnie enjoyed psychology more. She liked knowing how the mind actually worked, rather than how ancient philosophers said it should work. The one philosophy course Winnie had taken long ago in college made very little impression at all. Aristotle left her cold.

And Irina didn't jump in to say, *Oh, I love philosophers!* And so Macolm Benfry had to forge on on his own.

"It was from William James," said Professor Benfry.

"Do you know him?" He gestured toward Winnie. "I expect you do."

She did. "One of the first American psychologists," Winnie answered. "Late 1800s, I'd say."

"That's right," the professor said. "But he was also a famous philosopher. Brilliant man. Very compassionate. Do you know him?" he asked Irina.

She smiled. "I do."

Winnie felt a pang, as she so often did, realizing how much she still wished she knew. Irina spoke at least two languages, Russian and English, and she knew about an American psychologist and philosopher. Winnie doubted she knew even one Russian philosopher's or psychologist's name. The only Russian name that sprang to mind at the moment was Tolstoy. Winnie was glad there wouldn't be a test.

"Then perhaps you know this one," Professor Benfry said to Irina. "*The transition from tenseness and worry to equanimity and peace often comes about, not by doing, but by simply relaxing and throwing the burden down.*"

The professor paused. He widened his eyes at both of them. "So simple? *Throw your burden down...*" He shook his head. "Just wonderful. Changed my life that day. I thought, Mavis doesn't want me like this. Crying and carrying on all the time. I could hear her scolding me with that beautiful Scottish voice: 'Malcolm, throw that burden dooown!'" He chuckled at the memory of it.

"And so I became a new man in the garden," the professor said. "I still had my first attempt, roses dead and black and pests everywhere—but I started again in a planting bed right beside it. And for the rest of the summer every time I went out there to till and mulch and plant, I told myself first, *Malcolm, you throw that burden down.* And now do you want to see it?

This time both Winnie and Irina enthusiastically answered, "Yes!"

"First, look at before William James." Professor Benfry pulled out his phone and scrolled backward to the relevant year. "There are several. It just gets worse and worse." He passed the phone to Winnie and Irina to study while he finished the rest of his bagel sandwich, once again covering his mouth with his hand while he chewed.

He was not being modest when he said he had a black thumb. His rose bush looked like it had been run over, dragged, beaten, and torn. It was a wonder there were any green leaves on it at all. Winnie counted only three pale pink petals still clinging perilously close to death. That poor plant. Malcolm Benfry was, as he promised, a terrible gardener.

But his house, visible in the background—that was an utter delight. It looked just like a classic English country cottage should. With thick white walls, two chimneys, a white picket fence, an actual thatched roof—it was hard to believe the man sitting across from her got to live there, when clearly it was meant as a movie set.

"Your poor roses," Irina said, flipping through the rest of the pictures. "He did a show on them once," she told Winnie. "But I forgot how bad they were before." She handed the phone back to Professor Benfry. "Show her how they are now."

The professor patted his mouth with a paper napkin and began scrolling through his phone for more recent pictures. "Ah, these are lovely," he mumbled to himself. He passed the phone to Winnie.

An enormous pink rose bush had taken over the entire planting bed beneath the front windows. And, not satisfied with only growing horizontally, they had climbed up his front wall and spread over the top of the nearest window and continued on to grow over the top of the doorway and down the other side.

It created a rose-framed portal to the charming English cottage. Winnie could imagine the scent of them every time anyone passed in or out of the door. She scrolled through the pictures as she would have flipped through a magazine devoted to English country homes. What an unexpected treat on a day devoted to psychic experiments.

"You would say it's the soil," Malcolm Benfry said to Irina. "Yes?"

She smiled. "You know what I think."

Winnie stopped scrolling. She paid attention to Irina. "What do you think?" She had caught the professor saying Irina was a soil expert. Winnie had been so intent on his story, she didn't pursue any follow up questions about Irina. But now she wanted to know.

But it was the professor who answered for Irina. "She calls it my love garden," he told Winnie, "because I have poured so much love into my soil. Nothing else in my garden grows even a fraction as well. But Mavis's roses ... well."

Irina smiled. "I know what I know. Believe me or not."

"What is your field?" Winnie asked her.

"Soil science," Irina said. "Specifically soil remediation."

"She's a nut about it," said Professor Benfry. "Never seen a girl so in love with dirt."

Irina laughed good-heartedly. Winnie enjoyed how much the two of them seemed to like each other. They might be mentor and student, or colleagues, or simply friends, but they acted as comfortable and supportive with each other as grandfather and grandchild. They were a pleasure to be around.

Professor Benfry shrugged. "If you say Mavis's roses grow because of love, I will accept that. And I have to say, that exhibition just now with the dice ... obviously our feelings had an enormous affect. How many doubles did we all throw when we were sad and lonely and depressed because we couldn't talk to each other or even look at each other?" He shook his head. "Grief did not feed my garden."

"Throw your burden down," Irina repeated.

Malcolm Benfry nodded. "I had to." He smiled at them both. "Mavis would have had my hide."

There was a knock on the door. The lab assistant Geoffrey opened it and stuck his head in. "We're starting again, if you're ready."

Professor Benfry pushed back his chair and reached for Winnie's empty paper plate to stack on top of his own. An English gentleman to the end. He threw them both away in the trash can in the hall while Irina headed for the restrooms and Winnie went back to the snack room to fix a cup of coffee for Amanda.

Throw your burden down...

Had she? Winnie examined her own heart. And she knew the answer was no. But maybe *not yet*. Could she? One day? Yes, one day. But for now she was doing the best that she could.

She couldn't imagine Joe scolding her the way Mavis Benfry might have scolded her husband.

And if the roles were reversed, Winnie wouldn't have tried to hurry Joe along either. People felt what they felt when they felt it.

But she did lock away the conversation. She knew that hearing it had been meant for her.

The Magic of Timing was real, and maybe there was magic in being here today with these specific people. In fact, she was already convinced of it.

And the next experiment Amanda threw at them only reinforced what Malcolm Benfry had just told her.

Proof that the power of love was tangible and measurable—and real.

12

Winnie returned to the lab and handed Amanda her steaming cup of black coffee.

She also gave her one of the oversized chocolate chip cookies, wrapped in a napkin.

Amanda blew out a sigh. "Bless you." She took an immediate, hefty bite and washed it down with a swig of coffee. Winnie could almost see the sugar and caffeine molecules whip through her friend's bloodstream.

One of the many things Winnie appreciated about Amanda Birkauer was her appetite. Winnie assumed other triathletes like Amanda had all sorts of restrictions about what they ate and drank, but Amanda seemed perfectly content to eat whatever she wanted, when she wanted, and in as much quantity as she wanted.

It made it easy and relaxing to be around her. Because Winnie lived that way, too.

Their food-themed rituals extended beyond the annual Brain Day plate of nachos.

There were also pancake breakfasts at the Student Union on the first day of every semester. Italian or Chinese takeout when they turned in the last of their grades at the end of finals. All the various cakes Winnie made for Valentine's Day, St. Patrick's Day, Fourth of July, their birthdays. Cinnamon rolls for Christmas. Also sour cream coffee cake for Christmas, because you always had to have some of both.

And in between, whenever Winnie felt like it, a rotating roster of home-baked cookies. Chocolate chip, peanut butter, thumbprint cookies with Hershey's Kisses melted in the middle, peanut butter and chocolate chip together. Also loaves of banana bread and sourdough bread that tasted wonderful and made Winnie's house smell so good.

Winnie took great pleasure in keeping her friend fed. The way Amanda lived, she was always *doing*. Running here and there, training, teaching, running the parapsychology lab, running experiments through her ever-active mind, running in competitions, running for the joy of running.

Winnie the Labrador could only marvel at her friend the German Shorthaired Pointer. And nudge over with her nose her own bowl of kibble for her busier friend to wolf down.

Amanda finished her cookie, wiped her hand on the thigh of her pants, and took one more bracing chug of coffee. Then she shouted over the mingling conversations, "Okay! We all here?" She took a quick head count. All sixteen were back.

Winnie noticed the change in the room. For one thing, the craps tables were gone. And now in addition to the table that had already been set up this morning with movable dividers all along its length, Amanda and her lab assistants had installed dividers on the second table parallel to it, creating sixteen individual cubicles in all.

Winnie could see the closest one. A sheet of plain tan butcher paper had been taped down across the surface like a paper tablecloth. Once again Amanda and her lab assistants must have deployed box cutters to dissect cardboard boxes to make low barriers across the width of the cubicles. The dividers all along the table created barriers on the longer sides.

Amanda held up a small, round item that looked like a child's toy.

"Anyone know what this is?"

No one offered a theory.

"Okay, we'll get to that," Amanda promised. She closed her fist around the toy. "First, let me tell you a little story."

Her assistant Geoffrey sat at the end of the nearest table with a laptop opened in front of him. Amanda motioned for him to begin. Geoffrey clicked on the first image, which showed up on the large flat TV screen mounted on the lab's wall.

It was a picture of a baby chick.

"*Awww*, right?" Amanda asked, just as a few people made exactly that sound. What was it about baby animals? They stirred the heart. You just had to pet them. Winnie could never pass a puppy without stopping to stroke its little head and ears and lean in to smell its delicious puppy breath.

"Back in the old days," Amanda said, "the mythical 1980s—who remembers those?"

Most of the participants raised their hands. The Russian twins and the two lab assistants did not. Amanda shook her head at them. "So young. Anyway. There was a French research scientist named René Peoc'h. Anyone heard of him?"

This time no hands went up.

Amanda nodded. "It's too bad. But today we'll do him proud." She motioned for Geoffrey to click to the next image.

Winnie saw what looked like a chubby tin can sitting on top of a sheet of paper much like the ones taped to the tables right now. There were barriers around it, too, although they looked wooden, not cardboard.

"This is a robot," Amanda said. "Old-timey robot," she added for the younger set's benefit. "It's powered by a random number generator. We all know about those, right?"

This time heads nodded. Random number generators—RNGs—were common now in scientific research. It took the power of choosing random numbers away from humans who might accidentally skew the results of an experiment.

It was meant, among other things, to solve the Clever Hans problem.

Clever Hans was a famous horse in the early 1900s who appeared to be able to do math.

His owner was a German math teacher who taught the horse how to count and even do simple math equations. "Hans, how much is two plus three?" The horse would tap his front hoof five times. "Hans, how much is eighteen divided by three?" Clever Hans tapped out an answer of six.

People came from all over the world to watch the famous horse at work.

But eventually, as so often happened, someone made it his business to prove the performance was a fraud.

Not on purpose. No one was claiming that. But it was because Clever Hans was so bonded with his owner.

Every time Wilhelm, Clever Hans's human, asked

him a math question—and even though he wasn't aware he was doing it—Wilhelm would subtly and involuntarily tense when the horse reached the correct number.

So if Clever Hans were tapping out ten counts and the right answer was eleven, Wilhelm's body language somehow conveyed to the sensitive, intuitive horse that this next one was the right answer. Stop there.

Outrage, of course. Not toward Clever Hans and Wilhelm, but toward the German psychologist who felt it was his duty to crush the souls of happy people all over the earth by telling everyone he had solved this mystery.

But nobody wanted it solved. Couldn't they just have a counting horse in this world? What was wrong with the man? Go back home.

Winnie knew she would have been part of that group, despite her allegiance to the field of psychology. It was a topic that still came up now and then among her colleagues, even more than a hundred years later. Winnie had stopped debating it. She knew which side she was on. She only wished she had been able to see Clever Hans in action for herself. She could imagine how thrilling it would have been to nervously wait, holding her breath, while the horse methodically scuffed his front hoof against the dirt on his way to the correct answer.

Eventually, to the relief of many researchers,

someone invented the random number generator. Humans and sensitive horses could be taken out of the equation.

Now, instead of a human accidentally or intentionally skewing some scientific test result through body language or some other means, the RNG would act completely impartially by spitting out numbers at random and having everyone subject to them at the same time.

Winnie had her own experiences with them. As anonymous Test Subject 2143 of the University of Arizona parapsychology lab, back when she when was an absolute bear about keeping her clairvoyant abilities secret and making sure her fellow professors and her students never discovered her role in the mind lab's research, Winnie had spent hours reciting numbers generated by RNGs that she saw in her mind's eye and reporting them to Amanda or her lab assistants.

In other experiments, Winnie watched displays of numbers from an RNG and then sent the numbers telepathically to her partner, either sitting across from her or in another room. Once, in a test of long-distance telepathy, Winnie worked with another clairvoyant who lived in India. Both of them passed numbers back and forth mentally as if the miles between them meant nothing at all.

But that didn't look like the kind of experiment

Amanda was about to conduct. Winnie stared at the flat-screen TV for the next clue.

Amanda signaled to Geoffrey to bring it up.

The robot in the picture now lay on its side so everyone could see the tiny wheels on its base. But that wasn't the only modification. There was also the point of what looked like a ballpoint pen sticking out from the center of the bottom of the can.

"Next," Amanda told Geoffrey.

The robot sat upright up a sheet of paper and now there were lines covering the whole surface, looking as though the robot had drawn in boundaries and freeways and roads on some intricate map.

"The random number generator inside the robot directed it where to go," Amanda explained. "Every few seconds it issued a new command—this number meant go right. This was go left. Go up. Go back—and you can see from the lines the robot drew that it really does look random. Right? Okay, next."

And there was the fuzzy, adorable yellow chick again. But this time, sitting behind the wires of a tiny cage.

And fanned out behind it were several more baby chicks. Maybe ten or a dozen in all.

"Here's a thing about chickens," Amanda said. "And ducklings—you probably remember this from Psych 101. They imprint on the first moving creature they see when they hatch. Remember Konrad Lorenz followed around by all those ducklings?"

"Yes," answered a lot of the participants, including Winnie. She remembered it very well. It was adorable. This severe-looking white-haired old man strolling across the grass to a nearby pond, leading a little string of waddling ducklings who thought he was their mama.

Amanda gestured toward the picture on the TV of the baby chicks in their little cage. "See, this is where I just have pause and say, how did René Peoc'h even think of this? Because he came up with the weirdest experiment. When these baby chicks hatched, the first thing he showed them was the mini-robot. They thought that was their mother. He put the robot in their pen for a few days to let them really fall in love with it. That was their family now. Next."

Now the picture showed an overhead view of the way the experiment was set up. A tabletop covered in paper, bordered on the edges with strips of wood so the robot wouldn't fall off as it rolled around.

At one end of the table sat the cage holding the baby chicks that had bonded with the robot.

"Before I show you," Amanda said, "think about this. These are just a few days'-old baby chickens. Not exactly prized as scholars. Probably not a psychic among them. But they loved their robot mother. Keep that in mind. And remember, the robot is just a machine."

Amanda signaled for the next image. Again an overhead view. And a few seconds later, Winnie heard gasps. One of them was her own.

"Think about it," Amanda said, pointing at the lines the robot had made on the paper. "These baby chicks are in a cage, they're stressed, and what do they want? They want their mother close. They *made* their mother come close."

Winnie could see that Amanda was right. The lines on the paper told the story.

Now, instead of showing a crazy quilt of lines everywhere, right, left, up, and down—now all the lines were confined to just one area of the table.

The robot had gone straight from its starting position in the center of the paper, over to side of the table right next to the baby chick's cage. Then it's almost as if it paced back and forth in front of the chicks, always staying right where they could see it.

"What are you saying?" one of the British men asked. Winnie didn't see which one.

"I'm saying," Amanda answered, as animated as she always was when she talked about exciting ideas, "those baby chickens were able to move an object with their mind. Maybe not even with their minds—let's say it's just their emotions. They were afraid, they wanted comfort, and so *bam*—they reached out with their energy or their emotions or their minds and took control of a mechanical robot and brought it rolling right to them."

She let that sink in for a moment.

"So you're telling us," said the British man with the walrus mustache, "that those baby chickens performed psychokinesis?"

"I am telling you that," Amanda answered with confidence. "And what's more, I'm betting if baby chickens can do it, everyone here can do it, too. So let's find out."

A murmur went through the crowd. And then chuckles. And smiles. Winnie was smiling herself. Because Amanda was right about the experiment: How did someone even think that up? Winnie wondered that about a lot of different experiments. Did the scientist suddenly get some inspiration while taking a shower or doing the dishes or stripping wallpaper off a bedroom wall?

Winnie had the experience so many times of feeling mentally relaxed while doing some repetitious activity, and then suddenly some insight popped into her mind like toast popping out of a toaster. It always felt like a gift. She couldn't imagine how this strange and wonderful experiment came to René Peoc'h, but Winnie was eager to give it a try herself.

Amanda opened her palm and showed them all the toy she had teased them with earlier. It looked like a plastic blue ball the size Clover could carry in her mouth.

"This is a robot with an RNG in it," Amanda said. "You can get them online for about twenty bucks. We gave it a few upgrades…" She turned it over and showed them the wheels and the end of a mini-Sharpie sticking out from the bottom. "This is your mama," she told the group. "Your assignment is to keep her close to you."

Now Winnie understood the setup of the room. Sixteen individual work stations where they would all replicate the baby chick experiment.

Winnie caught Amanda's eye and laughed. Amanda gave her a little nod of recognition. She knew her friend would find this fun.

"Quick break," Amanda told them, "then pick your station. We'll do a test run with just the robots wandering around on their own, and then you'll sit down and send them some love."

Irina squeezed Winnie's arm on her way out of the room. Winnie remembered her question just in time to tug Irina back.

"Listen," Winnie said, "I don't know if you have any plans tonight…"

"Oh, very big plans," Irina answered. "Dinner, fall asleep in my room. Our bus picks us up at seven in the morning."

"How would you feel about a home-cooked meal?"

Irina sighed. "I feel I could fall down and kiss your feet."

Winnie laughed. "That won't be necessary. You're invited. I'm having Amanda Birkauer over, too."

"Thank you so much," Irina said, "but can we talk about it later?"

Winnie released her to run off again to the restroom.

She noticed Irina's twin, Max, did not seem to have that same problem. He had already found a station to claim as his own and was holding a lively conversation with the dowdy British woman who sat beside him.

Winnie grabbed the first empty spot further down the table.

She was happy to see Malcolm Benfry take the empty seat beside her.

"How did you start doing your gardening programs?" Winnie asked him. She knew as soon as she had time she would start catching up on all of them.

"Irina," Professor Benfry said. "You know the young people. Always want to video their own lives. *This is me eating an omelette. Watch me take this computer out of a box.*"

Winnie couldn't disagree. Although she often appreciated how granular some of the how-to videos online were whenever she needed help figuring out some tech issue with home appliances and anything else whose operation stumped her.

She had a bookshelf full of home repair books now —some of them very good—but sometimes nothing beat a three-minute video on how to reset motion detector lights or replace a leaky showerhead.

She always sent a silent thank you to those people for taking the time to teach her and anyone else searching for help.

"That sweet girl was very sick for a long time," said Malcolm Benfry. "Don't know if you knew."

Winnie shook her head. She had watched that brief scene of Irina in the hospital with Max crying at her bedside, but that was all. She didn't know any more. Even her experience inside the Vault didn't give her any information about what really happened.

"Spring came 'round," Professor Benfry said, "and I thought I might try something to cheer her up. My garden was a wreck, of course, but at least Mavis's roses were growing a little by then. It was a year after what I told you about at lunch. I thought maybe I'd learned a thing or two."

He settled back into his comfy Scandinavian seat, relaxed and in no hurry. A born storyteller.

"So I started from scratch," Professor Benfry said. "Dug up all the old planting beds I'd neglected since Mavis died, and I thought about what I could plant that would make Irina smile."

"What did you?" Winnie asked.

She hadn't noticed Irina return. But now the young

Russian took a seat at Winnie's other side and scooted her chair back enough to listen to their conversation without interference from the dividers between their stations.

"He planted *everything*," Irina said. "I think he bought every kind of flower they sold in the garden store. Then he planted them wherever he wanted, anywhere he saw some dirt. None of it made sense. Everything just grew every which way." She gestured wildly to demonstrate the chaos. Then she smiled. "But it was so, so beautiful. And yes, it did make me happy."

"I sent her videos," said Professor Benfry. "One every week. Explaining what I tried, what failed, what seemed to be doing all right so far."

"And they were so funny," Irina said. "The nurses couldn't believe it when they heard me laugh. They all had to come see why. They loved his videos, too."

Winnie found it hard to imagine that people were surprised to hear Irina laugh. In this brief half day of knowing her, Winnie had heard the young woman laugh countless times. And seen her smile. Always so ready to smile.

And yet, hadn't Winnie seen that Irina for herself? Kneeling on an iceberg of bright white light, so sad, so forlorn, hopeless?

Winnie wondered what had happened back then, and how Irina had climbed out of it to be who she was now.

"Okay, let's get started," Amanda called out to everyone. "We'll be coming around with your robots."

"I'll tell you more later," Irina promised. "He saved me. I can tell you that."

Malcolm Benfry waved away the sentiment. "You saved yourself, my dear."

Now Winnie really wanted to hear more. But Vella and Geoffrey were coming around to everyone's station with a box of round robots for the participants to choose.

"Don't just rush through this part," Amanda told them. "Try to get a feel for which of the robots will work with you."

Winnie saw the man with the walrus mustache choose a robot, hold it for a moment, then put it back. He picked another. Passed it from one hand to another. Then nodded at Vella. He'd keep it.

When it was Winnie's turn, there were four robots left in the box. One of them, the one on the furthest left, looked a little cockeyed. Maybe the wheels weren't on exactly straight. Or maybe the mini-Sharpie wasn't perfectly aligned.

Whatever it was, it called to Winnie. The way she might gravitate toward the runt of a litter. She didn't want the best one, the most perfect one. She wanted the one who needed her most.

That would be her baby chicken mother.

Amanda showed them where to turn them on.

"Now set them in the middle of your paper and just watch. Don't try to influence them at all."

Winnie set the little blue ball in the middle of her work table. A few seconds later, it began to move.

Its turns looked jerky. Very square and angular. Up, sharp turn to the left, down, another sharp turn.

The lines it made on the paper reminded her of the Etch A Sketch she had when she was a little girl. It was about the size of a notebook, and had a red frame around a blank gray screen. You'd turn the two white knobs at the bottom of the frame to draw what looked like charcoal lines on the empty screen. One knob drew vertically, the other horizontally.

Some of her friends became masterful at it. They could draw elaborate buildings and landscapes and even animals—although that was hard to do since the knobs drew only straight lines. But there was a way to draw curves if you learned how to manipulate both of the knobs at once.

Winnie just never got it.

And her runt robot probably never would, either, and that was okay with Winnie. They were in this experiment together.

And just that thought, that one brief feeling of affection toward her little robot, was enough to make it veer off its random course and start heading straight for Winnie.

She let out a laugh. Then stifled it. She wasn't supposed to do this yet. It was an accident.

But Amanda had been watching all of them from afar, and now she came toward Winnie to see what was happening there.

"Okay, everyone," Amanda said, "let's pause for a moment. Come look at this."

While the robots kept rolling around on the papers at everyone's stations, the people crowded around Winnie's station while Amanda asked her questions.

Amanda pointed to the straight aimless lines, then the direct line toward Winnie. The robot was still moving on the paper, but it was staying close to the side where Winnie sat.

"Why?" Amanda asked her. "What happened right before it did this?"

"I thought ... *we're in this together.*"

"Ah-ha," Amanda said with a smile. "There you go." She looked around at the group. "Anyone else couldn't help themselves throwing out some love?"

The dowdy British woman raised her hand. And so did Max. And Irina. And some others.

Now Winnie joined the group as they all went from station to station looking at other people's papers.

It was amazing. It was exactly like the pictures Amanda showed them of the baby chicks and their robot. Random lines, nothing to see here, and then *boom.* Suddenly the robot knew what to do with its life. Suddenly it had a purpose.

"I can see we need to adjust the experiment," Amanda said. She told Vella and Geoffrey to give everyone fresh sheets of paper.

"While they do that," Amanda said, "everyone come over here with me." She gathered them in the corner of the room, over where they'd stored the craps tables. "Turn your backs to your robots, please," Amanda told them. "No peeking. Obviously we need to be a little more strict."

People smiled at each other as they obeyed the newest rule. Like naughty school children who had been scolded by their kindly teacher.

"Now count backwards from two hundred by sevens," Amanda said. "We're going to have to occupy your minds."

Winnie was fine with the first few subtractions. Two hundred, one hundred ninety-three, on hundred eighty-six … but then she started struggling, had to use her fingers to count it out, while some of the scholars had no trouble at all and kept working their way down the ladder of numbers.

Malcolm Benfry was a wizard at it. He got as far as eighty-eight before Amanda released them.

"Okay, your robots have been just wandering around, doing what their RNGs told them to do—and now it's your turn. Go send them some love and see what happens."

Everyone eagerly returned to their stations. Like children turned out for recess.

Winnie sat in her sheltered cubicle and sent out her messages, this time intentionally.

Hi there! You're so pretty. You're the best robot out of all of them. Come over here and let me look at you. Yes! That's it! Come on now!

It came easiest when she thought of the robot as a puppy. Not as a mother at all. As something she would hug and nurture and protect. And her robot seemed to want that. It came straight for her and never left her side of the table.

Winnie could hear people laughing. And they weren't just sending messages with their minds. She could hear them shouting encouragement. Coaxing. Complimenting. Cheering when their robots did it right.

Too soon, Amanda called time.

Winnie looked at the clock. They had been playing with their robots for fifteen minutes. It barely felt like five.

Her paper was covered with black lines, most of them right in front of her, thick from going back and forth, back and forth.

"Well done!" Amanda told everyone as she surveyed the results of their session.

"Can I keep this?" Irina asked.

"The papers, yes, once we get pictures of all of them. The robots," Amanda said, "sorry, but no."

Sixteen adults groaned about losing their new favorite toys.

Winnie actually felt a slight pang of loss about it. How would she ever find another robot like it? She had bonded with this one. It felt special.

But a moment later she came to her senses about it. What was she planning to do with it anyway? Take it home and build it a little pen where it could roll back and forth all day? And then she'd feel like she shouldn't leave it, or it would just go all over the place randomly. How boring. But if she was in the room, it would come over to her side and roll back and forth until it got her attention.

Winnie chuckled at herself. It was madness. And it showed her what a great job Amanda had done of making them so attached to a plastic bit of hardware. She really did think of it as a puppy. One more thing she'd feel bad about leaving home alone for too long.

Winnie glanced at the clock again. It was close to 2:30. She was enjoying herself—they all were—but she wondered what Amanda's last experiment was going to be and how long it was going to take. Now not only did she need to get home to the dogs, she also had to figure out what to make for dinner tonight as a treat for a Russian visitor.

For a moment she felt tempted to invite Professor Benfry, too. She wanted to talk to him some more while she had the chance.

But the reason she wanted Irina to come to her house was to hear what she saw during their session in the Vault.

I need to apologize. For saying you were lonely ... about your husband Joe. The plane crash...

The plane crash. What could Irina possibly know about that?

As much as Winnie enjoyed talking to Professor Benfry, this was a matter of the heart.

And she wanted only Amanda and Irina there for that.

13

When Winnie returned from their short break, she found the lab rearranged again. Now the long tables had been moved over against the nearest wall, leaving an open space in the middle of the room. All sixteen participants stood in the clearing, still wearing their stylish wire wigs, wondering what was coming next.

What came next was Geoffrey the lab assistant hauling in a banker's box that looked like it might be heavy. Or at least heavy for him. Vella was probably stronger.

He set the box on the ground and waited for Amanda make the introduction.

"Okay, this is our last experiment everyone—"

A few groans, but also, Winnie noticed, a few

glances at each other in relief. The day had been exciting, fun, and also, she could see on some of their faces, exhausting.

She had no idea what other experiments Amanda had put them through the two days previously. The tests were never very physically challenging, but even brain work could wear a person down over time.

Winnie felt pleasantly tired, letting her know she had done something today. But she still had energy for whatever last treat Amanda planned to share with them all.

Amanda signaled to Geoffrey to do the next thing.

He removed the lid of the box and then dumped the entire contents onto the timeless linoleum floor.

Metal spoons and forks clattered into a heap.

Winnie smiled. She had seen a flash of this when Amanda called her yesterday to invite her.

"Anyone want to guess?" Amanda asked the group.

Two or three people answered at once:

"Spoon bending."

Then came the applause. Because everyone had heard of it, maybe some of them there had even done it before, and it sounded fun and frivolous—and, as far as Winnie thought about it, magic.

Amanda picked up a spoon from the pile and held it out for inspection. "These are not thin little cafeteria spoons," she told them. "These are nice, thick Oneida."

She passed it around so everyone could feel the thickness and the strength.

When it got to Winnie, she did what she saw the others do, holding the spoon in both hands and testing how easily it might bend.

The answer was, not easy at all. Winnie could feel a slight dip in her own confidence.

She wondered if any of the others might feel a little more daunted now.

"Anyone ever done it?" Amanda asked them.

The tall, thin British man with the questionable goatee smiled and raised his hand.

"Excellent, Edgar," Amanda answered. "Then maybe you can tell us the best technique."

The man's roots as an Oxford professor immediately shone through as he held out his hand for the spoon and then addressed this crowd of pupils. Based on the goatee alone, Winnie expected him to sound pompous.

But he was surprisingly modest as he began by saying he had been wrong about how to do it.

"I thought if I simply stared at it," he told them, holding the spoon in front of his face and almost making himself cross-eyed, "then it would droop over." He made an arc in the air with his finger, demonstrating how the spoon would just bend from the power of his mind. "But you do have to hold it both ends," he said, taking the bowl of the spoon between two fingers of one hand and the end of the spoon in the other hand. "Lightly, though. Not to bend with force, but just to feel for when the metal suddenly changes."

"Yes," Amanda said, leaning down to pick up one of the Oneida forks. "That's it exactly. And what are they waiting to feel?" she asked Edgar.

"A wet noodle."

Amanda laughed. "I was going to say rubber, but I like wet noodle better. Yes." She held the fork by its tines in her left hand and by the handle in her right. "When the moment comes—and you'll know it, I promise—you're going to feel the middle of it suddenly feel like a wet noodle. Then what?" she asked Edgar.

He seemed pleased to be her assistant. Winnie understood the feeling. It wasn't about showing off or being the teacher's pet, it was about the pleasure of sharing information with people who wanted to learn it.

That was at the root of any great teacher. The love of sharing what they knew.

Winnie realized she had misjudged Edgar when she saw him scowl about doing the experiment inside the Vault. Maybe he was claustrophobic. Maybe he was afraid he couldn't do it. Maybe he just didn't like that his partner for that exercise, Malcolm Benfry, had volunteered for them to go first.

Winnie always tried to guard against misjudging people. She tried to approach everyone with an open mind, giving them the benefit of the doubt. If she got a good feeling from someone, that was usually all she needed to know.

If she got a bad feeling, she might turn up her clairvoyant perception to check out their auras and gather more information that way. But she hadn't done that with Edgar. She'd just judged him based on his questionable facial hair and his scowl. But now that she turned up her own personal dial, she could see a lovely light green aura all around him.

Edgar was all right.

"Once you feel the metal soften," he continued instructing them, "you have to move right away. It seems to harden up again very quickly. Then you won't be able to bend it anymore."

"Care to demonstrate?" Amanda asked him.

The proper British gentleman actually blushed. "No, no, I couldn't…"

Amanda gave him an encouraging smile. "I think you could. Come on, no one here has done it. Please?"

"Please?" others asked. "Pleeease?" Then they laughed, knowing they sounded like whiny children.

But Edgar took it good-naturedly. He seemed to be gathering his courage. Winnie understood his reluctance. He might fail. In front of friends and colleagues and strangers. No one was anxious to do that.

"I can't look at any of you," Edgar said. "Let me…" He took his spoon and started wandering away from them. "Pretend you're not watching," he called back over his shoulder. "Sometbody sing something."

Max immediately accepted the challenge. He started singing. Not a Russian song—only Irina would have understood it. He picked a French song instead. The children's nursery rhyme *Frère Jacques*.

Soon others joined in. Including Winnie and Amanda.

Frère Jacques, Frère Jacques, dormez-vous? Dormez-vous?

That was the extent of Winnie's knowledge of the lyrics, but Amanda was able to belt out the song with everyone else, all the way to the end.

Or almost to the end.

Because just as they reached *Ding, dang, dong,* suddenly Edgar, who had been walking in a circle a short distance away, staring at the ceiling and holding his spoon lightly between both hands—Edgar suddenly cried out, "Ha ha! Got it!"

Then he turned to them all, delight written on his face, as he held up his misshapen spoon.

He had bent it in half at the handle, but had also pinched the thick round bowl together to make the sides of it flatten and touch.

Then he showed them that he couldn't move it anymore. He couldn't unbend it in any way, even when he applied strength to it. The spoon had frozen into that new configuration, and the magical noodle phase was over.

People exclaimed. People clapped. People crowded around him, desperate now to know exactly how he did it.

Amanda stood off to the side and let Edgar take the lead. Winnie caught her eye and saw how much Amanda was enjoying all of it.

After a few minutes of excitement, Amanda clapped her hands for order again.

"Okay, everybody! Your turn! Now you know it can be done, right?"

But then Edgar raised his hand. "If I may … I want to add that I took my spoon bending lesson with Cecelia. Some of you know Cecelia?"

A few British heads nodded.

"She's eighty-one," Edgar told Amanda and the rest of the group. "She's shorter than you," he said, pointing to Winnie, who hadn't noticed until then that she was the shortest in the group. "Well, she learned to bend spoons and forks that night, same as I did. But she didn't want to stop there. So they gave her a fireplace poker." Edgar mimicked twisting it into a pretzel. "Someone went out onto the street and brought back a piece of steel rebar from where they were repairing a building next door. Cecelia bent that in half, as if it were nothing. Utter madness. As if she had suddenly become a circus strongman."

Amanda's jaw hung open at that. "Wow. Okay, then," she told the group. "All we have are forks and spoons today. Sounds like it should be no problem."

"What were you doing while you were walking around in that circle?" Malcolm Benfry wanted to know.

Again, the tall, thin man with the goatee blushed.

"You'll laugh," Edgar said.

People shouted *No!* assuring him that they wouldn't.

Edgar looked around the group. Winnie wondered how many of them were his friends, not just colleagues. She tried to put her best, most empathetic expression on her face. She could see how easily Edgar might be spooked now, and she wanted the information as much as everybody else.

Edgar cleared his throat. He started mumbling. His voice sounded soft and sing-song and gentle. Winnie and the others had to lean in to hear.

*"Here, pretty spoon, here spoon, will you bend for me, pretty? That's right, that's a good girl, let's bend now, thank you, my love, thank you, lovely, that's right, my girl, come on now, let's **BEND!**"*

Edgar shouted the last word with so much unexpected force, people flinched and jerked away.

"You have to ask it," Edgar told them somewhat apologetically. "You have to shout at it in your mind. Although … it really works better if you shout it out loud. All at once. As a group."

Amanda grinned. "Wonderful. Thank you, Edgar. We'll do exactly that. Everyone, grab your utensil. Spoon or fork, whichever you want. I don't have a fire poker or any rebar. Sorry."

The Brits and the Russians and Winnie all fished through the pile of Oneida flatware. Winnie took out a sturdy-looking soup spoon. She had wanted a smaller teaspoon, but Amanda hadn't brought any of those.

But it was mind over matter, Winnie reminded herself. It didn't matter if it was a spoon or steel rebar. What mattered was the concentration of her mind.

"All right, everybody, let's spread out into a circle," Amanda said. Vella and Geoffrey stood on either side of the clearing, both aiming video cameras at the group.

Edgar had a new utensil, a fork this time. Most people, like Winnie, had chosen spoons. But both Irina and Max had forks.

"Bold choice," Winnie whispered to Irina, who stood beside her.

"Max took a fork," she whispered back. "I couldn't do less."

"What do you say, Edgar," Amanda asked. "On the count of three?"

The British gentleman nodded.

"Count three and then we'll all shout *bend*," Amanda instructed. She held her own spoon, ready to do it with them.

"Ready?" she shouted.

Then everyone shouted it at once.

"One … two … three … BEND!"

Winnie had been holding the spoon lightly between her hands, not bending it, not pushing or pulling or asserting any force.

And as her voice cried out with the others, **BEND!** —suddenly she felt it. The wet noodle. It made no sense. It felt bizarre. But it was absolutely real.

Winnie acted fast. She bent the spoon in the middle and, in a moment of artistic inspiration, gave it an extra twist while she could.

And then, just like Edgar said, it was over within two seconds. Winnie's spoon wouldn't budge for her, not in any direction. It was now bent backwards in half, with the bowl of the spoon twisted inward, kissing the handle.

In the background Winnie heard laughter. Laughter of amazement and delight.

She looked up to see what everyone else had done. People held up their flatware, showing it, sharing it, staring at it with disbelief.

Max's fork looked like a sculpture. He not only bent it in the middle, he also folded the two outer tines in and bent the two inner tines out, making them look like two sets of crossed fingers. The silver utensil now looked like something that could be sold in an art gallery. *Mystic Fork.*

Irina's fork was less elaborate. She bent it half, as they all did, then folded all of the tines down into a curve wide enough you could thread a pen through it.

The group oohed and ahhed over each other's creations, marveling that it actually worked.

But Winnie noticed one of them not showing her own work.

Amanda.

Winnie sidled up to her friend. "What's going on?" she mumbled.

"Nothing." Amanda took the spoon from behind her back.

Nothing, was right. The spoon looked exactly as it did before.

"Did you try?" Winnie asked.

"I tried."

"You never felt it?"

"I'm not sure," Amanda said. "Maybe."

"Well, let's do it again," Winnie suggested.

"We will. In a minute."

But Amanda, normally so confident in everything she did, sounded uncertain. Maybe deflated.

"It's a bad spoon," Winnie said, snatching it from Amanda's hand and throwing it away in the nearest trashcan.

When Winnie returned, Amanda gave her a reluctant smile.

"Come on," Winnie said. "I'll do it with you."

Now Amanda's smile looked more relaxed.

"All right, everybody," she called out to the group. "Let's go ahead and do round two. Pick out something new."

Winnie waited with Amanda while others sifted through the Oneida pile and found their next utensils.

"Remember what Edgar said," Winnie coached her friend. "You have to sweet-talk them. You can't just grab the first one and expect it to like you."

Amanda lifted an eyebrow. But she didn't fight the advice.

When she and Winnie took their turn at the pile, Winnie heard Amanda mumble, "Who wants to bend for me? Huh? How about you?"

She gently removed another spoon from the pile.

Irina must have been watching the whole interaction. Including Winnie grabbing Amanda's spoon and throwing it away.

She came now to stand with Winnie and Amanda. "I know the secret," Irina told them both confidentially. "Do it with me."

Irina had chosen one of the Oneida soup spoons this time. Winnie had moved on to a fork. Amanda held her new spoon, the one she felt bonded with from the pile.

Everyone else resumed their places in the circle. People were smiling, excited, ready to perform the magic again.

Winnie planned what she would do to create a design with her fork.

But first she needed to make sure Amanda could bend her own spoon.

"Ready?" Amanda called out.

Some people changed how they stood, getting into more of a runner's stance, as if this required speed or feats of strength instead of pure mental power.

"We will shout the Russian word for bend," Irina whispered to Winnie and Amanda. Then she pronounced something that sounded like *g'nees*.

They both quietly repeated it. *G'nees*.

Winnie and Amanda exchanged a look. Amanda looked upbeat again. Winnie was glad to see it.

"All right!" Amanda shouted. "Ready? One, two, three—"

And while the others shouted BEND! Irina and Winnie and Amanda shouted G'NEES! as the three of them waited to feel the magic wet noodle of their metals.

Winnie felt it right away. And so she acted. Bent the fork in half, twisted the outer tines outward—

And then it was over, and her fork would not move anymore.

She looked over at Amanda. Still nothing. Her new spoon looked exactly like before.

But Irina was not abandoning the effort. She had bent her spoon and twisted the handle, but now she took it between her hands again and told Amanda, "With me! One, two, three, G'NEES!"

Amanda shouted it. And then Winnie saw her eyes widen as she obviously felt what they all had felt.

Amanda bent her spoon in half, whooping as she did it, amazed at herself, amazed at the magic—amazed even though she was the one who set up this experiment in the first place.

Irina had used her second round of spoon bending to do what Edgar had shown them at the beginning. She pinched the thick bowl of the spoon together, flattening the sides of into an enclosed shell.

The two women held up their creations for the rest of the group to see. Applause broke out. Cheers. People congratulated Amanda and some of them seemed even happier for her than they were for themselves.

"One more time!" Amanda cried, pointing to the utensils still piled on the floor. "We have plenty! Keep the energy up!"

People grabbed more utensils. Winnie scooped up another spoon. And to the count of one, two, three, they shouted BEND! or G'NEES! and created their new sculptures out of sturdy flatware.

"You get to keep these," Amanda told them all, clearly treasuring her own two spoons that she'd finally successfully bent. "Let Vella and Geoffrey take pictures first, then those are your souvenirs."

Winnie looked at her three new pieces of art. Not as

elaborate as some that others—especially Max—made, but still a pleasure to behold.

And more than the fork and two spoons themselves, Winnie treasured that absolutely alien feeling of shouting to the metal and then feeling it respond in her hands. Melting for just a moment. Becoming a wet noodle. Because she asked it to. Because she bent her mind to it first, and asked the metal to respond.

That was real. That happened. She felt it. She had never felt something so strange and magical before. And to see everyone else do it, too. What a gift Amanda gave them. And Winnie could see on everyone's faces that they appreciated Amanda for doing it. For having the creativity and the organization and the resources to let everyone see what they were capable of doing.

"That's it," Amanda called out. "As soon as we finish your pictures, you're free to go. But thank you all so much for coming all this way and for giving us three days of your precious time. Give yourselves a hand! You've been amazing! WOOT!"

Everyone clapped and cheered for themselves and each other, and even the dowdy British woman joined in their collective response of "WOOT!"

Winnie gazed around the group with affection. These people had all been strangers to her this morning. Now she felt like at least a peripheral member of their tribe.

There was the usual commotion of people talking,

laughing, coming down from a mutual high. Vella and Geoffrey took photos of people holding up their misshapen forks and spoons, smiling with genuine delight.

Winnie remembered to find her little robot's two pages of scribbling. She still needed to think about that experiment and what it meant. For now, everything still felt like a blur.

A happy, magical blur.

Winnie glanced at the wall clock above her. It was 4:15. She needed to get home to Clover and Arthur.

But first she waited for Irina to finish whatever conversation she was having with her brother, then Winnie motioned for her to come over.

"Will you still come for dinner?" Winnie asked.

"I would love to come for dinner." Irina smiled with such warmth, Winnie could feel the joy radiating off of her.

"What would you like me to make?" Winnie asked.

Irina considered that for a moment. "What would you make for yourself tonight? If you didn't invite me over."

"No, that's too boring," Winnie said.

"But I like boring," Irina answered in her charming Russian accent. "I like to see people's lives. I want to see yours."

Winnie quickly made a mental scan of the groceries and pantry items she had at home. Could she really throw something together from those? Maybe. She might just have an idea.

"Amanda can pick you up at your hotel," Winnie said. "About six o'clock?"

"Good. I can pack and be ready for tomorrow." Irina leaned forward and gathered Winnie into a hug.

It seemed to be catching. Winnie saw the Brits and Max take turns coming over to Amanda and giving her a hug. They sought out the two lab assistants, too, but Winnie noticed Geoffrey shyly holding up his camera as if to block them. Vella took their hugs in stride.

Winnie gave and received her own share of hugs, and lingered over the one from Professor Benfry.

"I wish we could talk longer," Winnie said.

"I know," the professor answered. "I feel the same way." He smiled cheerfully. "But maybe you will come visit us in England some day."

Winnie didn't want to tell him she didn't travel much anymore. She simply smiled and told him, "I might."

And then an image flashed in her mind.

Of walking in Professor Benfry's garden among his wild and chaotic flowers with the fairy tale thatched-roof cottage sitting in the background.

Irina was giving Winnie a tour. Her dark hair was longer, past her shoulders now. She wore comfortable-looking light brown pants tucked into black rubber boots, and a cozy green and white wool sweater.

Irina was holding a baby.

And laughing with the tall, handsome blond-headed man at her side. He looked hardy, ruddy, outdoorsy based on his clothes. Canvas work pants that had seen some mud and grime in their time, what looked like hiking boots, and a black down vest over a dark blue sweater.

Irina and the blond man strolled at a pace Winnie could see was meant to accommodate Professor Benfry. He looked older, less mobile as he walked slowly with the aid of a cane.

Then the flash ended, and Winnie stood staring at Malcolm Benfry, her mind trying to deduce how many years in the future that scene might be.

"Huh," Winnie breathed out to herself.

But then she noticed that the professor still held her gaze.

He smiled, as if he might know what she saw.

"His name is Arni," said Malcolm Benfry. "She will meet him in three years. The baby is named Henri."

Winnie could barely hide her shock. Not that Professor Benfry was psychic, but that he hid it so well. Hid it from Winnie, when she thought she could usually sense the clairvoyants and intuitives around her.

Now she gazed around the rest of his group. "Are you all…?"

Professor Benfry surveyed the others, too. "Edgar,

of course. Madeleine" —the dowdy woman— "and Irina, you know—"

But no, Winnie didn't know. Not exactly. Although maybe she should have guessed it from what Irina said about the plane crash.

Professor Benfry named a few others. Winnie looked at them all with fresh eyes.

She remembered now what Amanda said when she invited Winnie to come join them for the day. *Not to make you competitive, but some of these people are going to blow your mind.* What else could Amanda have meant but exactly this? That among the Brits and the Russians were a least a few people who had extraordinary abilities?

Not everyone who came to the mind lab had psychic talents. Many were simply curious. *Tourists,* Amanda called them, and not unkindly. People who, for whatever reason, wanted to understand more about their minds' capabilities. It didn't mean they were psychic, it just meant they were aware. And that they wanted to do more with what their minds could naturally do.

They just didn't know what that was yet. Some of them came to the mind lab to find out.

And Winnie realized that was what she thought of these British visitors: *tourists.* But she had obviously been wrong. And she was happy to hear it.

"What experiments have you been doing the past

two days?" Winnie asked Professor Benfry. She hadn't wanted the information before, to guard against any bias or preconceived ideas, but the lab work was done for the day. Now she needed to know.

Malcolm Benfry ticked them off. "Clairaudience, clairsentience, clairgustance—"

Once again Winnie snorted like a fifth-grade boy.

"I tasted burnt broccoli Edgar was eating in another room. Blech." Professor Benfry stuck out his tongue in disgust. "And of course telepathy, precognition, intuitive diagnosis, mediumship, a few others—I expect you've done all of those yourself."

Not all, Winnie could have told him, and certainly not all of them in two days. No wonder Amanda ended their time at the mind lab with a day full of so much play.

"How did she even know about all of you?" Winnie asked. "I know she was at Oxford, but I've never heard her mention you before."

"Oh, I sent her a message," Malcolm Benfry said with a mischievous grin. "Telepathically. It took her a while—four or five months, as I recall—but finally one day she sent me an email. She said she'd heard about our little group—the Oxford Explorers Club. We were new, just a few years old. But still, were we interested in sharing some of our research?" The professor held out his palms as if presenting a delicious dessert on a platter. "As they say," he added with a chuckle, "*voilà.*"

Winnie shook her head in amazement. And delight.

She gave the professor one last hug.

"Well, it looks like I'll be seeing you some time in the next few years," Winnie said.

Malcolm Benfry nodded. "It does look that way."

Winnie knew that the future was always subject to change. People had free will. Nothing was set in stone until it actually happened. Irina might meet Arni some day, and, like Winnie had considered that day she met Joe, run away. Not step into that future. Same with having a baby. Right now little Henri was a possibility. Only Irina and Arni could create that actual future.

But Winnie could imagine a trip like the one that just flashed across her mind. Seeing the professor and Irina again. Meeting Arni and baby Henri.

And walking through Professor Benfry's riotously colorful English garden and later settling down for tea inside his quaint English house.

Visiting Mavis's roses. Malcolm Benfry's love garden to his wife.

Yes, that all might be a reason to go.

Winnie wandered back toward Amanda who looked like a captain at the helm of her ship. Surveying what needed to be done next, while also appreciating the stunning view from her deck. She looked satisfied. Winnie loved to see it.

"Happy?" she asked.

"Very." Amanda pulled out the two bent spoons she

had tucked over the waistband of her running pants. "Have I shown you these?"

"I don't think so," Winnie answered with a straight face.

"I did that," Amanda said.

"Really? That's amazing."

"It actually was," Amanda said with a trace of awe still visible on her face.

Winnie squeezed her friend's arm. She could only imagine how Amanda felt. To have watched these kinds of experiments for decades, but never actually tried any of them herself.

At least Winnie assumed that. But maybe she was wrong. Maybe Amanda had tried and just not succeeded until today.

Amanda Birkauer was right to hang on to her contorted spoons and show them off every chance she got. She had actually had a taste of magic today.

"Would you pick up Irina and come over around six?" Winnie asked her.

"What are you making? Not that it matters," Amanda was quick to add. "I'll eat your sofa cushions if you just soak them in batter first."

"I'll try to come up with something a little better than that," Winnie said.

Then with one more sweeping, grateful look at the people gathered in that room, Winnie slipped out. It was time to get home.

On the walk back through her neighborhood, passing the afternoon collection of dog walkers, some of which she also knew from the mornings, Winnie turned her mind to the mystery she still felt most anxious to solve.

She zipped up her purple fleece vest and dug her hands into her pockets. As the sun lowered, the late afternoon brought a welcome chill.

I'm sorry I said you were lonely ... your husband ... the plane crash ...

First Winnie would whip up some dinner and dessert for her friend and her Russian guest.

And then hopefully she would get some answers.

14

"Well, who is this?" Irina said as she crouched down just inside the doorway to Winnie's house.

The dogs swarmed her. With love. With excitement. And with the natural instinct of animals who knew when they had met an animal lover.

"Yes, yes..." Irina cooed, sitting down cross-legged on the living room brick floor to let Clover and Arthur have their full fill of her. Irina laughed and scratched ears and bellies and accepted with consummate grace Clover's well-aimed licks that might have made it past Irina's lips.

Arthur, gentleman that he was, simply wagged his entire body in a combination wriggle and crawl, and before long he had made himself a nest of Irina's lap while Clover continued mobbing her with affection.

"I can call them off any time," Winnie said.

"Do not dare," Irina answered. "I haven't had a dog for years. I miss them so much."

Clover spared some love for Amanda, too, who took her usurping as Clover's favorite person in stride. She fluffed up the fur on Clover's shoulders, kissed her on the smooth yellow forehead between her ears, then let the Lab go back to smothering Irina.

"And hello to you, too, sir," she told Arthur, giving his ear a scratch. Then she said, "I smell things," and followed Winnie back to the kitchen.

This end of the house had an open floor plan. The living room, a dining nook, and the kitchen all flowed from one to the other, so that Winnie, busy in the kitchen, could still see and hear her guests.

Winnie and Joe had bought this old house, built in the 1930s, shortly after they married. They added a few rooms and opened up the kitchen to make it lighter and larger and more cheerful.

The living room had a high ceiling made of dark tongue and groove planks between thick wooden beams. The floor was red brick, darkened with age now after so many years, and softened by several Oriental rugs in shades of dark blue and red.

Joe had done some woodworking in his later years, and Winnie prized the beautiful pieces he made. Bookcases and tables made out of dark cherry wood, Winnie's desk made out of walnut, and the trestle table Joe made for the dining nook out of the old weather-beaten, splintering door he salvaged from their front entrance.

The original part of the house, including the kitchen, had beautiful oak floors they covered in braided wool rugs that already felt cozy underfoot. But one of the kindnesses Winnie did for herself in the first year after Joe died was to replace all the rug pads with thicker ones that felt more loving to her feet. It was a small thing, but now when Winnie stood at her bathroom sink or in the kitchen, or when she walked across the living room or down the hall, she noticed how soft the rugs felt underneath her feet. It was an extra dose of comfort she was glad she had given herself.

Every few steps in the house, there was someplace comfortable to sit down and relax. A couch and love seat with pillow arms, perfect for human and canine napping. An old rocking chair that used to belong to Winnie's mother, along with a matching wooden footstool that Clover had chewed a little too mercilessly when she was a puppy.

While the grown Clover and her new brother continued adoring their Russian guest, Amanda grabbed a seat at the trestle dining table and set two items on top of it.

"Have you named them yet?" Winnie asked of the two misshapen spoons.

"Hortense and Greta," Amanda answered. "No, I haven't named them."

Winnie laughed. "It's okay to be proud."

"Tell you the truth," Amanda said, "I don't know what I feel. That was some actual woo-woo stuff there."

"You see woo-woo all the time," Winnie reminded her.

"Yeah, but I don't *do* it."

Amanda had changed into her off-work outfit, which looked suspiciously like her work one. Navy blue running pants with *Arizona* written down the side, but now in the colder evening, a red quarter-zip fleece sweater that had no University of Arizona branding on it at all. She was slipping.

Winnie wore what she usually did on cold nights: light gray sweatpants, warm socks and fleece-lined slippers, and an old soft T-shirt with a flannel shirt over it. And for now, a peach-colored apron she'd won at a raffle that said *Baking Makes Sense of the World*. Winnie couldn't agree more.

Irina stood gazing around the homey living room as she brushed off the hair samples the dogs had left behind. She had changed into black sweatpants and still wore her purple Princeton hoodie, both of which showed off Clover's yellow fur to perfection.

Clover and Arthur must have decided they had

sufficiently greeted Irina by now, because both had resumed their positions on the couch, lying tail to tail.

"I love your house," Irina declared. "I LOVE your house."

"Thank you," Winnie said with sincere appreciation. She loved it, too. It was exactly what she and Joe had made it to be.

At least partially de-haired, Irina joined Amanda at the table.

"I have a question," Irina said to Amanda. "Why are you surprised? Didn't you believe we could all bend spoons?"

"You, yes," Amanda said. "I mean, I've read about it, sure. I've seen videos of it. I know it can be done. And of course I thought all of you could do it. After what I saw the first day, I changed everything I was going to do today. I thought all of you were incredible."

"But you didn't think *you* could," Winnie said.

Amanda scowled and shook her head. She held up her hands, like she was surrendering. "I'm the sailor who can't swim."

Irina laughed. "I understand. I have an excellent grasp of theoretical chemistry, but I cannot—can *not*—do the lab experiments. They never work for me. Liquids explode. Equipment fails. I took terrible grades. My teachers could never understand it."

"Ever heard of the Pauli Effect?" Amanda asked.

"No," Winnie answered as Irina said, "Yes."

"Tell her," Amanda said.

"Wolfgang Pauli was a physicist," Irina answered. "German?"

"Austrian, I think," Amanda said.

"He won the Nobel Prize in Physics for … something," Irina continued. "But many of his colleagues banned him from visiting their labs. Every time he walked through them, instruments broke, equipment stopped working—"

"He was a menace," Amanda said. "One story I read was someone's equipment mysteriously broke, and the scientist said, 'Well, at least it wasn't Pauli this time.' They assumed he was nowhere near there. But later they found out Pauli had just switched trains at that same moment, and was in fact in their town for something like just ten minutes."

"Enough time to break things," Irina said.

"Woo-woo," Amanda said.

"So you think that's you?" Winnie asked Irina. The timer went off on the oven. Winnie held up her finger for them to wait while she grabbed her hot pads and pulled out the cookie sheet.

Amanda stood up to get a better view. She gave an approving nod. "Cookies for dinner. You won't be sorry," she told Irina.

"There's food," Winnie assured her Russian guest. She grabbed a spatula and started transferring the triple-chip—chocolate, butterscotch, and white chocolate—cookies to the sheet of parchment paper she'd laid on her granite counter.

"Anyway," Winnie asked Irina, "do you think there's a … I don't even know your last name."

"Tolstoi," Irina answered. "With an 'i.' No relation. We checked."

Winnie paused at that. It had happened more than a few times that some name popped into her mind, and she assumed she understood the reason.

At lunch, when Professor Benfry told Winnie and Irina his story about finding that passage from the psychologist and philosopher William James, Winnie realized she couldn't think of a single Russian name at that moment but Tolstoy. She assumed it was the writer.

But now she knew differently. It was Irina's name coming through.

Winnie returned to her train of thought. "Maybe it's the Tolstoi Effect," she told Irina. "Something about you interferes with chemistry experiments."

"Stick a pin in that," Amanda said. "If anyone ever writes a paper about it, I'm telling them that's what it's called." She rose halfway up from her chair to look at the cookies again. "Are they cool yet?"

"Can you wait two minutes?" Winnie said, familiar with both her friend's perpetual hunger and her impatience around Winnie's baking.

"Not really," Amanda muttered.

Another timer dinged. Just in time.

Winnie pulled out the baking tray from inside her toaster oven. She'd sliced off rounds of the honey-infused goat cheese she bought for some other recipe that she still hadn't made because she was missing a few ingredients. But she had a good use for it tonight. She lined the toaster oven tray with aluminum foil, then laid out the rounds of cheese and let them melt for a few minutes.

She had already made three bowls of salad. Now she set the melted coins of goat cheese on top of their lettuce, sprinkled a smattering of bright red pomegranate seeds on top, and could hear Malcolm Benfry's voice in her ear as she set the bowls in front of her guests.

Voilà.

Amanda sighed. "That's how it's done, son."

Winnie handed them a jam jar she'd run through the dishwasher once it was empty, and that now held a concoction of olive oil, balsamic vinegar, a smidge of honey mustard, and a little salt and pepper.

Amanda tested the lid and then shook up the dressing. She handed it to their out-of-town guest first.

Irina leaned over and smelled the greens and the seeds and the cheese. Then she gingerly added a few splashes of dressing, careful not to drown the whole creation.

Amanda was more liberal with the dressing, mostly,

Winnie could tell, because she was starving and just wanted to get on with it.

But Winnie had the satisfaction of seeing them both close their eyes and savor the taste and texture of the melted goat cheese.

That's how it's done, son.

Winnie had a few more steps to take care of before she could sit down and join them.

She took their drink orders: water or fizzy water? Ice or no ice? Unless someone brought it for themselves, there wasn't usually any wine in the house. Winnie had decided decades ago that she always wanted to keep a clear mind. Amanda liked to relax with a beer every now and then, but Winnie didn't have any on hand, and Amanda hadn't brought it.

Winnie poured filtered water for both of them and let them enjoy the rest of their salads.

Meanwhile she had an experiment of her own going on right now. She wasn't sure how it was going to turn out.

But in her experience, anything baked with puff pastry on top was a winner, no matter what was beneath it.

Like Amanda said, she would eat Winnie's couch cushions if she dipped it in batter first.

That was how Winnie felt about puff pastry.

On a cold night, it felt right to load up on root vegetables and cocoon them in a creamy sauce.

Winnie raided her vegetable drawer for whatever she had on hand. Carrots, onion, garlic, mushrooms, and two small red potatoes that she scrubbed and cut into small chunks.

She tossed them all with a little olive oil and some salt and pepper, then roasted them in the oven until the carrots and potatoes were just starting to get a little soft. No one wanted to bite into a creamy casserole and find crunchy vegetables inside.

She had half a pint of heavy cream left over from a pasta dish she had tried out the previous week. Which was not a keeper. But that was the point of experimentation. For every four that Winnie tried, there might be at least one she would make again and again.

Never Be Bored. Cooking new foods was part of the program.

While the vegetables roasted, Winnie concocted a sauce made up of heavy cream, a teaspoon or so of fresh thyme leaves she grew in one of the pots on her kitchen windowsill, a little salt, and several twists of freshly-ground black pepper. She simmered it until it lightly bubbled, then tasted it. Added a little more thyme. Simmered it and tasted again. That seemed right.

When the vegetables looked and smelled appropriately roasted, Winnie took them out of the oven and tossed them in the sauce. Then she poured them into a casserole dish, knowing that her next step would probably make everything she had just done hardly matter at all.

She rolled out a sheet of puff pastry dough she'd taken out of the freezer and allowed to lightly thaw.

Then she laid it over the casserole and sliced a couple of steam vents on top. Last, just to give it a nice golden crust, Winnie whisked an egg with a little water and brushed it on the surface of the pastry.

She checked the time. It wouldn't be ready when her guests arrived, but it should be done within half an hour after that.

Winnie slid the casserole dish into the oven and waited for the puff pastry to perform its magic.

And if it didn't work, she still had one sheet of pastry dough left, and she could quickly cover one of the sofa cushions with it and bake that instead.

But now, just as Amanda and Irina polished off their salads, Winnie eased open the oven door to check on the dinner's progress.

The top of it looked golden brown. Cream was bubbling up through the vent holes. It smelled divine. Winnie closed the door and reset the timer for five more minutes to let it finish browning in the few spots that still looked a little too pale.

But the scent of it had escaped. And this time the smell of baking cookies didn't overpower it.

Winnie heard behind her a soft exhalation followed by a few words in Russian.

She might not understand what Irina said, but Winnie did understand the universal effect of smelling something delicious. It reminded her of cartoons she used to watch when she was little, where the scent of something looked like a white, smoky ribbon that left some charbroiling piece of meat or a fresh-baked pie, and floated straight to a fox's or bear's nose.

"Five minutes," Winnie announced. Then she sat at the table with the other two and finally dug into her own salad.

The goat cheese had solidified a little as it cooled, but it still tasted decadent and delicious, especially with the bright, sweetly tart pomegranate seeds on top.

"Where else have you eaten this week?" Winnie asked Irina.

The Russian named Winnie's favorite Mexican restaurant, the one that supplied the Brain Day breakfast nachos and the bean burrito that needed a platter to hold it all.

"I told them to go there," Amanda explained unnecessarily. Of course she did. Winnie would have, too.

"Where else?" Winnie asked as she forked up more of her salad greens. She was pleased with the salad dressing, too. The whole thing had worked out well.

Irina chuckled. "Only there."

"The past two nights?" Amanda asked.

Irina shrugged. "It was good. Everybody liked it. I think they will go back there tonight." She gestured toward Winnie's oven. "But I am ready for whatever you're making." She leaned back against the rails of the wooden chair. "And to talk to someone new. I love my brother and my old professors and my friends, but..."

"I get it," Amanda said. "Too much of a good thing."

Irina patted her stomach. "Like the Mexican food."

Seeing the Russian touch her belly like that reminded Winnie of the flash she had seen of Irina carrying her baby.

Should she tell her what she saw?

Sometimes people wanted to know, sometimes they didn't.

But Professor Benfry had seen that future, too. And he was obviously close with Irina. Winnie would leave it to his judgment whether to tell her.

The oven timer buzzed. Winnie took out the casserole, now bubbling and golden brown.

"Now comes the hardest part," she told Amanda. "You have to wait five more minute while it cools."

"I disagree with that," Amanda said.

"I know you do." It was a conversation they had had so many times over the years. Amanda would rather burn her tongue and the roof of her mouth than have to wait the precious extra minutes before she could eat.

Irina seemed amused by their exchange. "How long have you known each other?"

"Twenty-five years," Winnie and Amanda answered together. "And almost another half," Amanda added.

They both knew the date. They had celebrated it with takeout from that same Mexican restaurant, followed by slices of carrot cake Winnie made for the occasion, even though neither of them had the space in their stomachs to take it.

"But I want to know about you," Winnie said. She pointed to Irina's purple Princeton hoodie. "Is that where you are now?"

Irina nodded. "Postdoc since last year. We're on spring break now. That's why we took the trip this week."

"And what about Max?" Amanda asked. "Where is he?"

"Also Princeton—the town," Irina said. "He was able to get a work visa. He's an electrical engineer."

"I can see how close you are," Winnie told her.

Irina smiled. "More than you know. I have some of his bone marrow. Now he says I owe him. A hundred million dollars. I can pay him a dollar a month."

Now they were getting to it. Why Irina was in the hospital. Winnie needed to know it all.

And no better way than to just ask it outright. "What was wrong with you?" Although Winnie already suspected.

"Leukemia," Irina answered, confirming it. The bone marrow transplant was the clue.

Amanda gave a soft grunt.

Winnie and Amanda had both known a professor in

the Psych department whose son went through it in his twenties. That young man, unfortunately, didn't make it.

But here was Irina, proof that leukemia did not necessarily get to win.

Winnie thought of the scene she and Irina shared in the Vault. How frail and ill Irina looked. The hopelessness in her eyes.

But then the way she clung to Winnie after hearing that Winnie had met her almost five years later—today. And hearing that she not only lived, but she would be healthy and vibrant and happy.

Winnie wanted to pursue it now. To start asking questions. To find out what happened to Irina—and from there, to find out everything she knew about Joe.

But the timer went off again and Amanda was out of her seat in a flash. Grabbing three plates out of Winnie's cupboard and fishing a serving spoon out of her drawer and generally being at the ready, although she waited for Winnie herself to do the honors.

Which Winnie was happy to do, despite the interruption. The evening was just beginning. They still had plenty of time to talk about all of it.

And Winnie was hungry, too. As well as curious to see how her new cooking experiment turned out.

She tapped on the pastry crust with the edge of her spoon to break it open and dig out the first portion. It looked right. It looked wonderful. It certainly smelled like the kind of cold weather comfort food she loved to eat. Winnie dished out three large portions onto the plates, making sure to give each of them a generous slab of the puff pastry on top. Amanda carried her own plate and Irina's back to the table.

Irina picked up her fork. With a sly side glance toward both Winnie and Amanda, the Russian held her fork lightly between both hands and shouted, "G'NEES!"

Winnie reacted instinctively, shooting out her hand toward Irina's to stop her.

"Only joking," Irina said as she let go of the tines.

It was enough to prompt Amanda to pick up first one of her misshapen spoons and then the other, to test again whether they really were frozen like that now. Winnie could see her strain as she tried to bend them back to their original shapes. But neither of the spoons would budge.

Amanda shook her head. "Amazing."

But then all conversation and hijinks stopped. They all took their first bites of Winnie's meal. In silence. To concentrate.

Amanda closed her eyes and gave off a sigh. That turned into something that sounded like, *Yuuuuuuum.*

Winnie had to agree with that. It actually was extremely tasty. She only wished she had had enough ingredients to make more of it. Enough to have left-overs tomorrow.

Although what was she thinking. Even if she had made a double recipe, there would be no leftovers. The night's servings were whatever fit in that casserole dish.

Irina reached over and squeezed Winnie's wrist. She said something in Russian. Then translated it for her: *I wish to marry you.*

Winnie laughed. Again the image flashed through her mind: that handsome, rugged man walking beside Irina in Professor Benfry's English garden.

Not so far away. Three years? Three years until that scene. But maybe Irina would meet him not long from now.

The romantic in Winnie wanted so much to tell her. But she also knew that the Magic of Timing was real, and Irina and Arni would meet when they should meet, and things would take their course from there.

Still, she felt so tempted to give Irina at least a hint. *Oh, I don't think it's me you're going to marry...*

Winnie restrained herself. As she so often did when she caught glimpses of the future. Unless it was something dangerous like a washed-out bridge, in which case she shouted it right away.

Amanda ate like a football player now, shoveling it in so fast it was a wonder her taste buds had a chance to register anything.

But after the first flurry of hunger-fueled speed eating, she did manage to slow down, savor it a little more, and then once she cleaned her plate, to slouch back against her chair and let out a groan of satisfaction.

"I'll need seconds in a minute," Amanda said, "but that was—" She kissed the tips of her fingers and splayed them outward like a cartoon chef in an Italian restaurant. "Perfection. Seriously, thank you. That was outstanding."

She stood up and made good on her promise to serve herself a second helping.

Irina was still working on her first, taking her time, Winnie could see, to actually taste every single bite.

And then suddenly that slowness made Winnie feel antsy inside. As if Irina might have misunderstood the night's agenda. This was not just a social visit with a home-cooked meal. Winnie had questions. Lots of them.

So she might as well lay the foundation right now. "I have so many questions," she told Irina.

"Me, too," said Amanda.

"And me," Irina told them. She ate the last two bites and then shifted her plate away.

"More?" Amanda asked, already eating her own more.

Irina waved it away. "Later. Yes."

"And there's cookies," Amanda reminded her.

Irina laughed. "I will not starve here. Thank you," she told Winnie.

And in the composed, mature expression on Irina's face as she said that, Winnie could see a kind of old-worldliness about her. Something much older than her years.

Yes, she could be playful and fun. She could laugh and joke and tease.

But there was a seriousness Winnie could see behind those dark, intelligent eyes.

Irina had seen hardship. She had been through an illness that most likely tried to kill her. And maybe there were other dark moments bchind the light, joyous woman she appeared to be now.

Winnie had visited Irina during just such a dark moment.

How that moment led to this one ... Winnie needed to know.

15

Dr. Amanda Birkauer, Assistant Director of the university's parapsychology lab, had her own way of doing things.

And Winnie was glad of it.

Left on her own, she might have eased into it more, asked Irina to narrate the whole history of her illness, asked side questions, spent hours at it—because Winnie was genuinely curious. She wanted to know more about Irina and her life.

But Amanda Birkauer had a different focus. And it was exactly why Winnie had waited to talk to Irina until Amanda could be with them.

Because Amanda honed in on the real questions for the evening:

What did Winnie see in the Vault?

What did Irina see?

And why were they entirely different?

"I already reviewed Vella's notes of what you told her," Amanda said to Irina. "Winnie hasn't seen them. I'm the one who did Winnie's debriefing after your Vault session, so I already know about that. But Winnie, why don't you tell Irina what you experienced?"

The three of them sat in the living room now, having eaten their fill of the puff pastry casserole and the triple-chip cookies Winnie had baked.

Bringing out another satisfied sigh from Amanda. *Yuuuuuum.*

Winnie offered everyone tea, mostly to warm them, but Amanda declined and got up from the table and went straight to her favorite chair, the dark blue lounger, and plucked a fleece blanket out of the basket nearby to tuck in around herself. She was set.

Winnie waited for Irina to pick her spot. As if sensing their opportunity, the dogs shifted apart on the couch to make room for Irina in the middle. She took it. There was a blanket draped over the back of it, and Irina laid it over her lap, holding up the sides in case the dogs wanted to come under it with her.

Arthur took her up on it. The little dog was always colder than Clover, who waited for Irina to settle in, then laid her chin on Irina's thigh.

Winnie took the love seat. With a fleece blanket of

her own. She kicked off her slippers and sat cross-legged with her sock-covered feet tucked under her thighs. She arranged the blanket all around her and tucked that in, too.

It felt like they were about to have Story Time, these three adult women, all tucked in with their blankets and ready to listen.

Or in Winnie's case, ready to tell.

She paused a moment to gather her thoughts.

"Just start at the beginning," Amanda coached her. "What was the first thing you saw?"

Winnie sank back against the love seat and closed her eyes. She let the images find their way back gently into her mind. Trying to force anything was never good. Winnie relaxed and waited to describe what she saw.

"Irina is kneeling somewhere," she began. "On something very, very white. It looks like an iceberg. Or a slab of white marble. There's golden light glowing all around her. The light looks warm to me, like soft sunlight, but I can see Irina is shivering and very cold."

Winnie paused. Let the images grow clearer in her mind.

"Good," Amanda said quietly. "Go on."

"She's wearing a hospital gown. She looks very pale and thin. I say her name. She looks at me. She seems confused, or upset. She says something to me in Russian, but I don't know what."

Now Winnie felt that word drift across her mind once again. Wispy, without any real substance to it. Just a thought of what it sounded like, along with an idea of what the word meant.

"I think it was *help*," Winnie said.

She heard Irina's intake of breath. There in Winnie's living room, not in the mini-movie playing across her mind.

Part of Winnie understood that Irina was sitting nearby, no doubt tense and hanging on every word.

But to be faithful to what she saw, what Winnie experienced in that booth, she needed to block out the present and keep her mind in the past.

Amanda asked quietly, "What else do you see?"

Winnie waited for the images to mature in her mind. Then she felt what she did. What she thought. What she said.

"I'm sending her love. And healing," Winnie said. "I'm not sure if Irina can feel it. She's still shivering and looks so sick. But then she looks at me. Right into my eyes. And asks me if I'm here for her.

"I tell her yes," Winnie went on. The images were bright and clear now. She could tell her story without hesitation. "I keep sending her more love. More energy. I can feel it now. It really is going to her. I think I can even see it."

It was a shimmering, nearly invisible ribbon in the

air between them. More of a visible vibration than something more solid.

"Irina is looking at me," Winnie said. She could see the young woman's dark and pleading eyes. That desperation. "She needs my help. She feels so lost. So hopeless. She's certain she's going to die. But I tell her she doesn't. I tell her I've met her—five years in the future. Although I get a message it's really four years and ten months. I tell her she's strong and healthy then, and so happy. I promise her she survives."

Winnie could hear a sound nearby. A soft and quiet cry. But she had to stay with the other Irina in the vision. That was the Irina who needed her now.

"I need to get to her," Winnie said. "She's all alone out there. But she's too far. The water between us is too deep."

"What happens now?" Amanda quietly prompted.

"I ask for help. I need to get to her. I reach out my hand. She reaches out hers. Then I'm next to her. I can hold her. She's shivering and so afraid."

The sounds in the living room persisted. Irina sniffling. But Winnie pressed on.

"I tell her it's all right," Winnie said. "I'm hugging her now. She's crying, but I think she knows."

"Knows what?" Amanda asked.

"That she'll live," Winnie said. "I can see myself now. I'm dressed as a doctor. That's why she believes me. She looks so happy now. And relieved..."

Winnie suspended her story, content to simply watch the rest of the movie.

But Amanda must have suspected that was happening, because she butted in again.

"What's happening now?"

Part of Winnie's mind bucked at the intrusion. Why couldn't Amanda just leave her alone? Winnie wanted to watch the end of the movie in peace.

But another part of her knew she needed to continue telling the story. It was her duty. To tell it all the way to the end.

"Irina says…" And Winnie repeated a phrase—in Russian. Words she didn't know, in a language she didn't speak.

"I tell her…" And again Winnie spouted off a quick phrase in Russian that she didn't understand, but had no trouble pronouncing.

She heard a light gasp. Followed by a few quiet words in Russian.

This time the spell was broken. Winnie opened her eyes. She took a deep breath. And looked at Irina.

Tears slid down the young Russian's cheeks. Her hands were clasped tightly in front of her mouth. But Winnie could see the smile in Irina's eyes. Even as the tears continued to flow.

"What did she say?" Amanda, ever the researcher, asked Irina.

Winnie wanted to know, too. She had spoken the words, but they meant nothing to her.

Irina swiped her purple sleeve under her eyes and composed herself before speaking.

"She said I told her, *Thank you, Doctor*. And then she said…" and here, Irina's voice caught again, just for a moment. "She said, *Spring will come, little bird*." Irina smiled, a tearful, sweet smile. "It was what my father called me. Little bird."

She pulled the blanket off her lap and extricated herself from the dogs. Then she came over to Winnie and leaned over and hugged her hard. Whispered the word Winnie knew meant thank you.

Winnie hugged her back, relishing the feeling of Irina's strength and vitality now, instead of the emaciated young woman whose ribs Winnie had been able to feel as the younger Russian in the vision shivered in Winnie's arms.

But that wasn't the end of Irina's story. She had more to tell.

She returned to the couch and carefully settled back down between the napping dogs.

She took a moment again to steady herself. Like a diver standing at the edge of the high dive.

"You said it was four years and ten months," she said to Winnie. "That was the future you came from. Today."

Winnie nodded. Her arms goose-bumped. She

could feel something coming. She just didn't know what.

Irina's dark eyes glistened. She looked from Amanda to Winnie. There was color on her cheeks, a light bloom of rose.

"Four years and ten months ago I was in a hospital," Irina said. "I had cardiac arrest. My heart stopped. For over ten minutes."

Irina waited for it to sink in, to make sure they understood.

And with a thud of realization, Winnie knew that she had been wrong. When she first met Irina, she saw a mini-movie of Max crying beside her hospital bed. Irina was gravely ill. Winnie knew that much. But she also knew that Irina survived.

Winnie had purposely ended the movie there. She didn't need to see Max or Irina suffering. Too sad. And besides, obviously she knew how everything turned out.

But Winnie's interpretation had been wrong.

You almost died, she had said to Irina.

I did, Irina answered.

Winnie thought the Russian was confirming what Winnie said. But she wasn't. Irina was correcting her.

This time, Winnie got it right.

"You died," she said.

"I died," Irina said.

16

They needed cookies first. A replenishing dose of sugar. Some water. A mug of vanilla chamomile tea for Winnie, a mug of lemon ginger tea for Amanda. A bathroom break for all of them.

Just a few minutes of nothing so all three of them could relax. Winnie's mind was swirling. She imagined Amanda's and Irina's were, too. They all needed a little time to catch up with themselves. To let the swirling sand that had been kicked up in their mental waters come together again and settle back down to the bottom.

Irina, too, wanted a mug of lemon ginger tea. Winnie set the timer again to let it steep for six minutes.

Six minutes, and they would be back on duty again.

Until then, Irina petted the dogs, who woke up just to enjoy it. Amanda checked emails and texts on her phone. Winnie wiped down the kitchen counters and loaded dishes into the dishwasher.

The timer buzzed. Winnie squeezed Irina's tea bag over a spoon, added a small glop of agave syrup to the mug, and brought it out to her guest.

Then Amanda turned off her phone and put it on the coffee table. She took one last gulp of tea and set the mug beside it. Winnie sat back down on the love seat and tucked her blanket around her. Amanda tucked her own. Irina held the mug—a souvenir from Seattle, showing the Space Needle—between her hands and blew on the surface and took a sip.

Stalling. Winnie could see it.

She understood. How do you begin to talk about something so big? *Yeah, so I died—what did you two do that day?*

But Dr. Amanda Birkauer, ever the professional, always curious, always ready to explore, asked the right question to help Irina get back on track.

"Did you know you were dead?"

"Yes," Irina said.

"How?"

"I could see the doctor and nurses using a defibrillator on my chest. I saw the heart monitor. It was a flat line."

"Where were you?" Amanda asked. "When you saw that?"

Irina took another sip of tea. She nodded, as if that was a question others had asked. "At the side of the bed. Watching. I stood between two nurses. They blended with me. They didn't feel me there, and I didn't feel them."

"Over ten minutes, you said," Amanda continued. She wasn't taking notes, but Winnie knew she was cataloging all of these details in her head. When Amanda returned home tonight, she would write up notes from the whole evening. That was how she did it. She didn't like to take notes during an informal conversation like this. She wanted people to feel free to talk, without any nervousness because someone had suddenly taken out a pen and paper or recorded it on their phone.

But Winnie knew that Amanda's mind was sharp, and every single answer Irina was giving right now would be set down accurately in Amanda's research files within the next few hours.

"Fourteen minutes," Irina said.

"I wonder…" Winnie interjected.

Amanda shifted her attention to Winnie. "About the time in the Vault."

"Yes," Winnie said. "Exactly."

She and Irina had been instructed to spend ten minutes each sending healing and energy to the other.

But when the lights flickered to indicate ten minutes had passed, Winnie kept on going. She could see Irina needed it.

And here was some proof that she did. At least four more minutes.

"Now here's a question," Amanda said to Irina. "You heard everything that Winnie said. Do you remember any of that happening? Do you remember her at all?"

Irina studied Winnie's face. "I want to say yes. I feel I should remember her. But ... no. I don't think so. Not truthfully."

"But I can tell you," Amanda said, "when Winnie walked into the lab this morning, you responded to seeing her. You seemed happy. It did seem possible you knew her."

Irina shrugged. "I'm sorry. I don't really remember."

Now Amanda turned back to Winnie. "What about you? Did it seem like Irina was dead?"

Winnie considered the question. Tried to feel her feelings from back in the Vault. She added in her inner sight to try to give herself a deeper perception. But her answer was much like Irina's. "I really don't know. I think ... no. I didn't know. I just knew that she was very, very sick. And very sad. Lonely and afraid."

"That was how I saw you when I sent the healing," Irina said. "Not afraid, but lonely and sad. A very dark feeling all around you. I felt sorry for you."

An unexpected lump formed in Winnie's throat. To

hear Irina speak so plainly. *I felt sorry for you.* Even though the words were sympathetic, they made Winnie's heart sink. She could feel her own energy ebb away. Even though Irina was obviously extremely kind and empathetic, sharing such a blunt assessment of Winnie did not feel uplifting. Not in the least.

"We'll talk about what you saw later," Amanda told Irina. Winnie's mind relaxed with relief. She wanted to know everything Irina could tell her about Joe—everything. And yet, now that the moment was close, Winnie felt a tinge of fear about it. It might not be good news. It might be, like Irina said, dark.

Maybe it was better to put it off. Just a little while longer.

Winnie was surprised to feel that way, but she couldn't deny that she did.

Thankfully, Amanda still had plenty of questions.

"Tell us everything," Amanda said. "Start at the beginning. You knew you were dead. You saw yourself…"

"I saw myself lying in the bed," Irina said. "The doctor used the defibrillator. Twice. My heart was still dead. The line on the monitor was flat.

"But it was boring to stay there," said Irina. "So I decided to look around."

She sounded so casual about it. As if she were at a party and stuck with talking to someone dull. So she just moved on. Circulated. Saw what there was to see.

"Once I left them, it all looked gray at first. Just walking through a gray fog. That, too, was boring. I thought about turning back. But then I came to another room."

"How much time had passed?" Amanda asked.

"Time was … there was no time," Irina answered. "Centuries. Weeks. It didn't matter. I didn't feel it at all."

"Could you see yourself?" Amanda asked. "Did you have a body?"

Irina thought about it. "I knew I was myself. I wasn't a blob of light or something like that, if that's what you mean. I don't know if I looked at myself. I just was."

Amanda nodded. "Okay, go on."

"This room," Irina said. "As soon as I walked in, I knew it was different. It had no walls, but I knew it was a confined space. Set apart from the gray fog. Even though inside it was gray, too.

"But as soon as I stepped in there, I felt…" Irina paused. Looked up at the dark wooden beams of Winnie's living room ceiling. Searched for the right words.

"I felt very *certain*," Irina said. "I felt … that right now, I could know anything. Anything in the world—even the universe. All I had to do was ask myself—or maybe ask the room, I'm not sure—any question I wanted to know, and I would have the answer immediately."

She paused again, waiting to see if Amanda understood.

"So, it was like a … an information chamber?" Amanda asked.

"No," said Irina, clearly struggling to pin it down. "More of a … truth chamber. An *absolute* truth chamber … maybe." She sighed in frustration and turned to Winnie. "When you know something, through your clairvoyance—"

She and Winnie had never talked about it explicitly, about Winnie being clairvoyant, but obviously Irina knew it by now. Winnie had revealed it the moment she told Irina she saw Max crying at her bedside in the hospital.

"—are you absolutely certain of what you know?" Irina went on. "Do you see everything?"

It was an interesting question. Winnie had to think about how to answer. "I know what I see is true," she said. "I don't question it. But I don't see everything, no. I don't know everything. I see images. Mini-movies sometimes. I get feelings. Or information will suddenly drop into my mind."

Irina nodded. "So think of what that feels like … but this was more. Much more."

Winnie wanted to understand, but she didn't. Irina could see it on her face.

"Here," Irina said. She closed her eyes, and in the next instant, Winnie's mind had joined in the experience. As if Irina had hit *Copy, Paste.* Suddenly Winnie could see it.

"Oh…" Now Winnie closed her eyes, too, and she relaxed into the room. Irina's room. Winnie stood alone in a gray space, just as Irina had described. She couldn't see any walls, but she knew the room had limits to it. Somehow it was contained.

And it felt … the opposite of the Vault. Instead of the air in here feeling flat and dead, muting any sound, the room shimmered with a subtle energy. Not visible, but palpable just the same. An invisible static that in the physical world might have made Winnie's hair stand on end, like rubbing a balloon over it to build up a static charge.

"What's going on?" Amanda asked.

Winnie realized she and Irina had both been silent for some time. Winnie brought herself back to the moment. "All right," she said, "let me try to describe it."

The energy in the room continued to build. And now Winnie thought she knew what the room was for.

"It feels like a virtual reality room," Winnie said. She paused for a moment. "I just asked to see my mother. I don't know why. But that was the thought that came. And now I can see her. She's about twenty. She's wearing an old shirt, button-down, like a man's, and faded jeans rolled up at the bottom. And a big straw hat. She's kneeling in her garden, working on it with a trowel."

And what was so astonishing about the moment—admittedly, a very small, insignificant moment—was that Winnie was right in it. Both watching her mother and feeling what it was to *be* her mother. Listening to her thoughts. The list of other things she wanted to get to that day. Thoughts about a date she was going on that night. With someone named John.

Not Winnie's father. Her mother hadn't met him yet. Winnie somehow knew that, too. Just from feeling inside her mother's mind.

It was a strange combination of telepathy and clairvoyance and absolutely accurate virtual reality, like watching a 3D movie where she could slip in and out of the action on the screen. Both *be* the movie and watch it.

"What's happening now?" Amanda broke in. Winnie realized she'd forgotten to keep up her narration.

"Let me try something else," Winnie said, and it seemed right to ask about Amanda.

"You're riding a bike," Winnie said, watching as Amanda did. "You're eight, I think. Wearing flip flops. Blue gym shorts and a white T-shirt, with a bathing suit under it. You're going to swim practice. Your T-shirt says…" Winnie squinted with her mind. "San Rafael Swim Team."

"Are you talking about *me*?" Amanda asked her.

"Yes." Hadn't Winnie already said that? But maybe she'd only thought it. "It's very early in the morning. Your parents aren't up yet. But they don't really care what you do. They don't really like you—"

"Jeez," Amanda muttered.

"—so you just go to swim practice every morning in the summer, then you stay at the pool all day with your friends. You never have any money, but they let you come back to their houses and have lunch with them there, or they buy you snacks at the snack booth—"

"I see it, too," Irina said. "Her swim coach is named Debbie. The bottoms of her feet are very cracked from being so dry—"

"It's always so cold when they first have to dive in," Winnie said. "But once Amanda is in there—"

Both Irina and Winnie said it together. "She loves it."

"She might want to be an Olympic swimmer," Winnie said. She could feel that longing in Amanda's heart. Winnie's eyes remained closed. She was poolside watching Amanda swim laps with the rest of her team, and she was also sharing Amanda's mind. Thinking and feeling what she thought and felt.

"But how will she ever get the money?" Irina asked at the same moment Winnie, too, felt that thought in Amanda's mind.

"Okay, that's enough," Amanda said sharply.

Winnie opened her eyes.

She heard the bite to Amanda's tone. Saw now the look on Amanda's face.

Pain. Shame. Sadness. All in the flash of a moment. Then it was gone. Amanda looked calm and composed again.

But Winnie had seen it.

"I'm sorry," Winnie said, and she meant it. She would never want to cause her friend pain. The information had kept pouring into Winnie's mind and she simply kept reporting it as it came. But it was too much. Too personal. Too true. She understood that now, away from it.

"I'm sorry, too," Irina said. "Sometimes I know I go too far—"

Amanda waved them away. "Don't worry about it," she said with what looked like a normal smile.

It reminded Winnie of her own exchange with Irina that morning, after their session inside the Vault.

I'm sorry I said you were lonely. That wasn't kind of me...

Now she understood what Irina must have felt.

Because now Winnie had had that same pure experience. She knew the truth. She had watched it. No interpretation required. She had seen inside young Amanda's mind. She had felt what the young girl felt.

And it was so easy to report it as it happened. As if these were just facts, and anyone would want to hear them. Plain, emotionless facts, like reading off the items on a grocery list.

But now, away from the experience, Winnie understood perfectly well why Amanda didn't want to hear more. This wasn't a happy memory for her. Even with all of her success and the happiness in her life, obviously the wounds of Amanda's childhood remained. There to be re-opened if someone kept digging at it.

Amanda was right to stop them.

Maybe as a peace offering, maybe just to assuage her guilt, Winnie did Amanda a favor now.

Because she could see that this was now past the threshold of casual conversation. There was too much new material. Amanda must be itching to write it down.

So Winnie got up and dashed into her office in the next room, and brought back one of her pastel blue legal pads and a brand new pen. She offered them to Amanda, who seemed grateful to take them.

Winnie settled back down on the love seat, and Amanda, properly outfitted now, resumed.

"So explain it to me," Amanda said to the two of them. All business. All researcher. "You were in a room. Some kind of all-knowing, virtual reality room."

"Not virtual," Winnie said, now that she heard the word again. Yes, it had been her own description at first, but now she saw that wasn't true. "It *was* reality."

Irina nodded. "I agree. I have gone there many, many times now—"

"Wait a minute," Amanda interrupted. "You have? Even after this experience we're talking about?"

"Yes," Irina said.

Amanda wrote that down. "Okay, we'll come back to that. Go on."

Irina continued. "What I see and feel in there is always the truth. For good or bad. When you go there, you can ask anything. But prepare to know it all."

And it occurred to Winnie that this, for many people—including her—could be a kind of paradise. *The* Paradise. Heaven.

To have all information. For someone curious, wasn't that the ultimate gift? To be able to ask any question, to want to know anything about a person or event—and then get to see it in its true, original form? Without interpretation by someone else. Without the shading of opinion. Just raw truth. About anything, throughout all time.

Heaven.

Or, Winnie could imagine, for some people it might be Hell. To have to see what was true, to have to experience it from someone else's emotional perspective.

To have to experience someone's pain, maybe even knowing you were the one who caused it. To have to feel the petty disappointments and the deeper wounds you left trailing behind your careless life.

Was all information good? Winnie knew it wasn't. There were many facts she would never want to experience first-hand. Any kind of suffering. There was a limit. She recognized there truly was such a thing as too much information.

Meanwhile Amanda had stopped writing and now leaned back in her chair. Winnie could see she was thinking about what she heard. And her researcher's mind was busy at work trying to bring some order to it all.

"You died and you went to that room," Amanda said.

"Yes," Irina said.

"How long did you stay?"

"Again," Irina said. "I can't say that. Time meant nothing. I could have been there for two seconds. Or years. It isn't a proper measurement. Although … I do know they were still trying to make my heart start again. I saw that later."

Amanda nodded. Wrote it down.

"So you knew it was an information room," Amanda continued. "A truth chamber. You somehow knew that when you entered. What happened next?"

Irina took a moment to gather her thoughts. Then she offered them a little background.

"First, I should tell you that I have always been interested in World War II," Irina said. "I don't know why. Maybe I…"

"Lived through it," Winnie finished for her. That was a whole other topic. Winnie had her opinions about past lives, and so did Amanda. Irina probably did, too.

But this was already enough of an exploration. Amanda held them to the topic at hand.

"So what happened next?" she asked Irina.

"I thought, well, if I can know something, I would like to know what it was like to be an RAF pilot in World War II." Irina shrugged. "I have always been curious."

Winnie could understand that. Over the years she had seen her share of movies about the men in the Royal Air Force. They always seemed so brave and romantic.

"And what happened?" Amanda asked.

"Immediately. He was there."

"Inside the room with you?" Amanda asked, scribbling on the notepad.

"No," Irina said. "I was with him. Inside the cockpit of his plane. I knew his name. Robert Cleary. I knew who his family was. His dog, Clarence. His sweetheart, Maggie."

"Did he say anything?" Amanda asked.

"Not at first," Irina said. "At first he just noticed me. He didn't seem surprised to see me. There were two other men in the cockpit. A co-pilot and a navigator. I don't think they saw me. They never looked at me. But I didn't care. I was only there for the pilot."

"I know what you're saying," Winnie interjected. "When I was watching you," she told Amanda, "at swim practice, there were people all around, but I only cared about you."

"Did I seem to notice you?" Amanda asked.

Winnie thought about it. "No."

Irina agreed. "I don't think so."

Amanda nodded, taking in the information, but not writing it down. Maybe mentally she shifted it into whatever pile she thought it belonged in. In any case, she didn't let it distract her from the pilot.

"So what happened with Robert Cleary?"

"I felt very close to him," Irina said. "Like I was his best friend. And I could feel he was very comfortable with me. So I asked him, *Are you scared?* He said *yes, every time. You'd be a fool not to.* I knew he was out hunting for German planes. I asked him if he hated the German pilots. He said no, he hated Hitler, but he didn't hate the pilots. They had a job to do, same as he did. But he knew he had to shoot them down first, or they would shoot him. And he didn't want them to bomb his people. He felt very strong about that. He wanted to do whatever he could to protect them."

"So he told you all this," Amanda said, still trying to keep up and write it all down. "Were you talking in words? Or thoughts?"

Irina considered that. "If I asked him questions, he looked at me and answered. But sometimes I just knew what he was thinking. I could … *be* him."

Winnie nodded. "Same with my mother. I watched her from outside, but some of the time it felt like I was her."

Winnie almost didn't say it, because she didn't want to stir up bad memories again, but Amanda was a researcher. She needed to know it all.

"I was you, too," Winnie told her. "Some of the time, while you were swimming."

Irina nodded. "I as well."

Amanda paused. Looked at them both.

"Irina," she said, fixing her gaze now on the Russian. Winnie could hear a certain tone in her voice. She wondered what Amanda was about to say. "I have been working with you for the past three days, yes?"

"Yes," Irina agreed.

"Many, many hours," Amanda said.

Irina agreed with that, too.

"You are leaving tomorrow. I may or may not see you again."

Now Winnie knew exactly where this was going.

So did Irina. She smiled sheepishly. "I'm sorry. I apologize." She added a few words in Russian, maybe in further apology.

Winnie understood the issue perfectly. If she had

not wanted to talk to Irina about what she said about Joe's plane crash, she probably wouldn't have invited Irina and Amanda for dinner.

Which meant that none of this would have come out.

Amanda never would have heard of the information room—the truth chamber—or about the ability to watch and be Winnie's mother and young Amanda herself, or anything about the RAF pilot—none of it.

And now, whatever else Irina was about to tell them, that would have gotten on the bus with Irina tomorrow morning and disappeared without ever being revealed.

Winnie understood Amanda's frustration. And also the fear behind it. There was always so much more to know about all of this. If Amanda weren't constantly vigilant, it could slip through her hands and she would never, ever know.

And how sad that would be. For Amanda, for Winnie, for everyone. Irina's experience should be known. Should be shared. This was a story of a fellow human being who had experienced something extraordinary.

It was Dr. Amanda Birkauer's job to discover information exactly like this.

Not only her job, her passion. Her obsession.

So it wasn't surprising that Amanda sighed theatrically now and muttered a colorful curse that made both Irina and Winnie suppress a smile.

But then Amanda let go of her irritation. She had done the proper scolding. Now it was back to business. All of this was too important.

"You're with Robert Cleary," Amanda prompted. "Maybe you are Robert Cleary. So what happens now?"

"I … left," Irina said.

"You left? Why?" Amanda asked.

"I felt the conversation was over. I asked him my questions, he told me his feelings … that was what I wanted to know."

But Winnie could see there was more. Irina looked down at her hands. She seemed reluctant to continue.

"Why did you leave him?" Amanda asked softly. Maybe she already suspected the answer.

"I felt…" Irina looked up at both of them with her dark, soulful eyes. Maybe asking for understanding. "I thought … or I knew … he would die that night. I didn't want to feel it. I didn't want to know any more."

Her confession hung in the air. Winnie did understand. It was a hard thing to feel. After this intimate connection, to know the man's life was almost over.

But Amanda saw something different in Irina's answer. "You were there in his present, but you could also see his future?"

Irina thought about it. "I don't know. That's a good

question. Maybe I felt his dread. Maybe he was the one who knew his future, and he was telling me."

"Wow," Amanda said, slumping back in her chair. "I mean, this is all so…"

"Crazy?" Irina said with a smile.

"Fantastic," Amanda said. "Thank you for all of this." She picked up the legal pad and resumed her illegible scrawling.

"I have a request, though," Irina said, turning to Winnie. "More cookies, please. More tea. What time is it?"

Winnie looked at her watch. "Nine-thirty." Much later than she expected—but what was time? Normally she would be in bed by now, reading a book. Maybe even already asleep. But Winnie wasn't tired. Not sleepy-tired, anyway, although she was a little mentally fatigued.

She could keep going with this as long as Irina could keep it up.

Amanda was right. It was utterly fascinating. If Irina were staying another day, they might suspend the evening now and resume tomorrow. But this was it. Their best chance. The Russian was leaving in the morning.

Winnie went to the kitchen to prepare a reviving snack. Not just more triple-chip cookies, but also two pears cut into wedges, and a bowl of almonds, and some Triscuits and chunks of cheddar cheese on a plate. It was the best she could do without having gone to the store. And what little was left of the casserole wasn't enough to feed any of them more than a few bites.

She refilled everyone's mugs with tea. They all took their bathroom breaks. Winnie woke up the dogs and took them outside to pee.

This might take a while, to hear what else Irina had to say.

Winnie certainly hoped so. The day had already been full to the brim with discovery after discovery.

Why stop now? Let it carry them through the night.

They paused to eat, to drink, to reposition themselves under their blankets. Clover groaned and settled her chin back on Irina's lap. King Arthur, on her other side, curled up again right up against her thigh.

Amanda picked up the blue legal pad and pen. "Did you see anything else in the truth chamber?"

"No," Irina said. "I left then. I thought I should go back and check on my body."

Winnie's skin tingled. How often did someone hear a sentence like that?

"And what did you see?" Amanda asked.

"I was still dead," Irina answered. "They were still trying to start my heart."

Winnie could picture it. Clearly. Irina pale and limp. Her body arching in response to the jolt from the defibrillator paddles. The screen on the monitor showing her heartbeat, still blaring out its warning. No heartbeat. No life. Try again.

"So it was time for me to decide," Irina said. "There I was. Should I live or should I die?"

"You chose to live, obviously," Amanda said.

Irina shook her head. "I did not."

17

Winnie and Amanda both stared at Irina. They must have misheard.

"You did not choose to live?" Amanda asked.

"No," Irina said. She sighed. "Let me explain."

She sat up straighter on the couch. Clover groaned again. Too much jostling. But Irina had the look of someone ready either to testify or be tested. Her spine was erect. Her head held high. Ready to speak the truth.

"My life up to then was …" She splayed out her palms, as if in apology. "Not so good. I made many, many wrong choices."

"How old were you?" Amanda asked.

"Twenty-eight."

"Where were you? What were you doing?" Amanda asked.

"I was studying Medicine at Oxford," Irina said. "My parents paid for Max and me to go there so we both would become doctors."

"But you said Max is an electrical engineer," Winnie said.

"Yes. The defiant one. He changed early in our studies, but I still followed their wishes. Even though I wasn't interested, either."

"What did you want to study?" Amanda asked.

Irina smiled. And there it was again, that joy Winnie found so contagious. As if a light had been turned on inside of Irina's soul.

"Plants. Soil," Irina answered. "I have such a love of plants, it is almost too much to bear sometimes. Their beauty … it is so rich. So divine. I eat them and I feel I can become them. I touch them and I want to dive into their stems and their roots and just…" She hugged her arms across her chest and gave a sigh of pleasure. Followed by a laugh. "I warn you, this will all sound very strange."

Amanda smiled. "That's fine with us. Say whatever you want."

Now Irina opened her arms wide as if wanting to embrace the whole world. "It's a feeling of … total love. Total oneness. I never, ever felt that way studying medicine. But then I took a class from Malcolm Benfry—"

"Oh," Winnie said. "That's how."

"How he became my friend," Irina said, "yes. My mentor. My guide. My wise old man. Like an old wizard." She laughed again. "He doesn't like it when I call him that, but I am telling you."

Winnie could see it. That kindly old British professor in his rumpled clothes and with the wide, easy smile.

But also with abilities. That telepathy he surprised Winnie with by sharing his vision of Irina and Arni and baby Henri in the future.

The clairvoyance that provided him with that vision in the first place.

Irina was telepathic, too. She had proven that by including Winnie in her exploration of what the truth chamber could do. The next thing Winnie knew, she was seeing—and being—her mother when she was twenty. She was seeing and being young Amanda on her swim team.

Winnie knew she hadn't done that on her own. It was Irina who made it possible.

So if that was what Irina found in Professor Benfry —yes, it would have changed her life. Made her want to change it, at least.

But Winnie still didn't know the steps that led from

Irina flatlining in the hospital to this Irina she saw now.

She watched Irina, her dark eyes alive with wonder as she described it.

"I saw my body," Irina said, "lying there in the hospital bed. And I felt such..." She closed her eyes. Searching for the right words. "...such love, yes, but also such disappointment. Sadness. That I had allowed myself to become someone I did not want to be."

She turned to Winnie. "I think that was the Irina you saw. So sad. So sick. At the end of an unhappy life."

That sounded true to Winnie. It matched the pitiful young woman she met inside the Vault.

"Do you think it mattered, then," Winnie asked. "What I said to you? That I knew you survived, and you were so happy and well?"

"I don't know," said Irina. "But how could it not? You must have given me hope. At the exact moment when I needed it."

Winnie could hear Amanda's pen scratching on the legal pad. Taking down every word. Winnie wanted to remember every word herself. Everything that Irina was saying felt like a story Winnie needed to hear.

Their life experiences, their backgrounds, were so different. Yet Winnie felt an affinity with the Russian. A connection beyond just meeting her for the first time today. Something older. Deeper. Someone she was meant to meet, and meant to know now, going forward.

Irina went on. "I was very angry in my life. Defiant." She pressed her fist to her chest. "In here, but not to my parents, not to anyone. I was a good, dutiful child."

"Not a child," Amanda pointed out, "at twenty-eight."

Irina smiled wryly. "You do not know my parents. Very, very strong. I love them, but they have ideas about how I should be, how my brother should be—how everyone and everything should be. They do not release them lightly.

"But in that hospital room, it was just me … and me. A dead girl on the bed. Me standing there looking at her.

"I fell in love with her. I felt such compassion. Such an ache. So much pain for how she was living. I knew what she wanted … what I wanted … but I knew we were afraid. And yet here we both were, on the brink of life or death.

"I knew it was completely in my power."

"Your death," Amanda said.

"And my life," Irina said. "If I chose it, I was choosing it for me. For her. And it meant…" She searched again for how to put it. "It meant I was giving myself this gift of my own life. I could feel how much love I poured into my heart. I loved myself so much in that moment. I wanted to help her. Help me. I was the only one who could do it.

"And so," Irina said, "I knew I had to let my own life go. I had to leave that girl where she was, dead. Erased. And if I chose to go forward, I had to decide right now: Did I want to pick up that dead girl again and carry her the rest of my life, or could I leave her there forever and choose to walk away?"

Irina was silent for a moment. Winnie could feel her own heart beating. She barely breathed. The room felt electric. Alive, charged, the way the gray reality room—the truth chamber—felt charged with unseen energy pulsing through Winnie's veins.

"I knew," Irina said quietly, "that my anger was a dead end. My sadness was a dead end. All my worries, dead. I could not pick them up again. They belonged to the dead girl. I did not want them to belong to me.

"But I did want to live. I wanted my own life now. Not hers, anymore, but my own. Doing what I wanted. Living how I wanted. Loving my life. Loving it completely, for the very first time."

There was a joy to her voice. Winnie could hear it. She could feel it. She watched Irina share some of her love by running her hand down Clover's head and threading one of the dog's soft ears through her fingers. She cuddled Arthur's smaller, softer body closer to her leg. She was touching life, and letting life touch her. Letting the joy of life be hers.

"What happened?" Amanda asked quietly. Just enough to hear the words without it breaking the spell Irina cast.

"I let her die," Irina said. "I gave up her heart. I told her goodbye. And then I started my own heart. This new one." She pressed her hand against her chest.

Irina sent the vision of it to Winnie: the doctor looking at the time, about to mark it and pronounce the Russian girl dead. It had been fourteen minutes. They had tried so hard. But this young woman was not meant to live.

And before the words could leave his lips, Irina had become who she wanted to be. She had decided how to live now. She inhabited her old body and gave it the spark it needed to come back to life again.

Winnie looked over at Irina. The young Russian's dark eyes shone with unshed tears. And the smile she gave Winnie … that genuine, complete smile of hers made a pathway straight from Irina's new heart into Winnie's own.

Winnie looked across their small circle to Amanda. She, too, seemed transformed by what she had heard. Winnie could see a look of wonder on her friend's face. A look of calm and satisfaction. And maybe more.

Deliverance. A feeling of liberation. To be given something new that she had never heard or understood before.

And still Irina's words echoed in Winnie's mind.

My anger was a dead end.

My sadness was a dead end...

Winnie got it. She recognized it. Like a puzzle piece slipping into place.

It was exactly as Professor Benfry had said. The scolding he got from his wife Mavis to help him rise up out of his grief.

"You threw your burden down," Winnie said.

Irina smiled. And nodded. "I threw my burden down."

Winnie lay her hand over the puzzle inside her mind and in her heart, and she could feel for the first time a new smoothness to its surface. As if the ragged edges around the hole Joe had left were now filled with a piece Winnie didn't know existed and had never known to search for.

To have come from this woman who had been a stranger just hours ago.

But who couldn't be a stranger. Who was meant to be here right now, sitting in Winnie's living room, nestled between her two dogs.

If the Magic of Timing was real—and Winnie had seen proof of that, time and again—then everything from Malcolm Benfry reaching out to Amanda Birkauer with his mind, to Amanda inviting the Oxford group here—and even further back, to Irina Tolstoi meeting Professor Benfry and recognizing the path he represented—

To Irina choosing life. To Joe Parsons crashing his plane over the dark cold ocean. To Winnie agreeing to help her friend in the parapsychology lab…

And at least a dozen other pieces to this. Too many for Winnie to catalog right now. She felt drained. But also energized. Both at the same time.

The only sounds in the room were the dogs' quiet breathing and Amanda's pen scratching across the page.

Winnie slid the tips of her fingers beneath her glasses and rubbed her weary eyes.

This was enough. A full banquet by any means. There was no room for more. Winnie's mind and heart were completely full.

And yet…

And yet.

This wasn't all there was.

Winnie still needed to know one more thing.

Should she ask it? Was it greedy of her? After all that Irina had already given?

But this amazing young Russian woman would be on a bus in a few hours, and Winnie would be left wondering what she might have said.

If Professor Benfry's vision was right, Winnie would be seeing Irina and the professor and Arni and baby Henri in about three years.

But Winnie wasn't willing to wait that long.

"I know," Irina answered, before Winnie even

formed the words. She gazed at Winnie with kindness in her eyes. "You ask me about your husband. I will tell you now."

Amanda looked up from what she was writing. Winnie remembered Amanda saying she had read Vella's notes after the session in the Vault. So maybe she already knew what Irina would say.

And Winnie could read those notes for herself, even if Irina left now and they never saw each other again.

But right now, in this electrified, magical moment, Winnie hungered to hear it directly from Irina.

"Your husband died, too," Irina said. "He made a choice, too. To come back to you. To meet you. To share the love you both could have.

"He knew he would die again," Irina said. "Just as I know. When it comes, I will willingly go. But I am grateful that I have my life—so grateful. I chose it. I am living it with all of my heart every day.

"And that was how your Joe felt," Irina said. "He chose to keep living. He chose to come back. Because he knew what was waiting. A life with you. That he could live with his whole heart."

Winnie's eyes clouded with tears. Her lips trembled. Not with grief. But with a smile that felt like it belonged on another woman's lips. She felt too small for this joy. It was larger than she could take in. She had to let it come to her in just sips, slow and small, so it wouldn't drown her with too much emotion.

She wanted to ask questions. She couldn't. She couldn't find the words.

But Irina must have heard them. Understood them. She gazed at Winnie with love and compassion in her eyes.

"It's all right," Irina told her. "Everything is how it is. How it should be. How your Joe knew it would be. He and I both made our right choices." Irina beamed. "And look, I got to meet you, too."

18

It was after midnight. Winnie couldn't remember the last time she had stayed up so late.

She had walked Amanda and Irina out to Amanda's car and hugged them both goodnight. Hugged them hard. Irina kissed Winnie on both cheeks. Once again Winnie felt younger than the Russian. Her student, not her teacher.

The night was clear and cold. A half moon hung among stars glittering in the dark sky. Winnie let the dogs out one last time, then brought them to the bedroom to settle in for the night. She took a long hot shower, dressed in a flannel nightgown and warm socks, and climbed into bed to claim the narrow space left between the bed-hogging dogs.

Despite the late hour and the fatigue in her body

and brain, Winnie lay awake still thinking about every-thing Irina had told her.

Including the last bit of information Amanda squeezed out of their guest before Irina rode off into the sunrise in the morning.

"What did you mean," Amanda asked her, "about what you told Vella in your debrief after the Vault? You said you sensed certain things about Winnie."

Winnie didn't really need to hear anything more about Irina seeing darkness around her and knowing Winnie was lonely. Hadn't they already covered all of that?

But Winnie respected her friend's scientific method, and if Amanda needed to clear up some detail for her research files, Winnie wouldn't interfere.

"Ah," Irina said. "Yes. Inside the Vault it was like my truth chamber. I could feel you, Winnie. For a time, I was you."

She paused. And Winnie could sense Irina trying to decide how much and what to say. Now Winnie was curious. What exactly did Irina know?

But instead of talking about Winnie, Irina told them about herself.

"My life isn't perfect," Irina said. "Sometimes I'm angry at someone, or I can't sleep because of my worries. And when I realize it, I think, *Do you want to pick up that dead girl again and carry her on your back? Or do you want to be free?* And so I lay her back down.

Because I chose my life, not hers." Irina looked at Winnie. With a gaze full of compassion. "And I think you are allowed to choose, too."

Clover groaned and stretched out closer to Winnie's side. Little Arthur lay curled up on her right. They wanted her warmth. And Winnie was grateful for theirs.

This was her life now.

Lay your burden down.

She thought of what else Irina said, about her life before this one. The one she chose to leave behind her.

My anger was a dead end.

My sadness was a dead end.

And about Joe, and the life he chose.

He knew he would die again. He chose to come back. Because he knew what was waiting. A life with you. That he could live with his whole heart.

And he had lived it. Winnie had lived it with him. For as long as they could. With all of her heart.

Joe had chosen life. Just as Winnie chose life. She chose it every day.

She wasn't ready to be done. There was still so much more she wanted to learn. And she had friends and family and dogs to love.

But she understood what Irina meant. About choosing which life to live.

The old one, with the extra burden Winnie carried?

Or a new one, after she set the burden down?

Winnie rolled onto her side and spooned the yellow Lab stretched out beside her. Even in his sleep, little Arthur adjusted his position on her other side and snuggled up closer to fill the momentary gap.

And in the morning Winnie awoke after just a few hours of sleep, because the sun still came up when it wanted and shined into her bedroom and reminded everyone it was time for dog walks and breakfast and another day.

But first Winnie got to enjoy her first cup of coffee of the day while sitting up in bed, still warm underneath her covers.

Winnie looked at her bedside clock. The bus would be coming soon to pick up the Russians and the Brits and drive them to Sedona. Beautiful Sedona.

But that wasn't the life for Winnie today. That wasn't the one she wanted.

She wanted this one, with all that it was. From sunup to sundown, all of this life.

The old one was wonderful. She had created it with love. Like a mold she made exactly how she wanted, then had poured herself into.

But now that old mold was broken, it couldn't hold her anymore.

She needed to make a new one, and pour herself into that.

A mold that fit her life the way she could love it now. With all of the parts she had been gathering over the last three years. She still loved Joe. She always would. He was the love of her life. That would never change.

But Joe chose life. And Winnie did, too. And this was what it looked like. The sun still came up every day. And Winnie's life went on, the way that she made it.

She knew that creating her new mold might still take time. And that was all right. It was like any art that was worth the effort.

But there was a lightness to it now that hadn't been there the day before.

Sometime in the night, without knowing how she did it, Winnie had laid that burden down.

19

"I have a confession to make," Amanda Birkauer said as she and Winnie watched Clover roll in the frosty grass in front of the basketball stadium.

"You don't really like these cookies," Winnie guessed.

Amanda snatched the bag of them from Winnie's hand before she could take them back. "No, these I will defend with my life."

She bit into her second one. Rich with cream cheese mixed into a shortbread dough, with a swirl of strawberry jam. Winnie had invented the recipe the night before on a whim. But she kind of liked it. It could be a keeper.

Amanda wiped her mouth with the sleeve of her University of Arizona jacket. Which matched her U of

A running pants and the U of A cap that her long brown and gray-streaked ponytail was sticking out of.

Winnie knew she only had a few minutes of Amanda's time. They had interrupted her long Saturday run.

But as soon as Clover spotted Amanda at a distance, her tail started wagging, not just side to side, but in a complete circle—that special wag that Amanda called the corkscrew and that showed how much the Lab loved her. Then there was no keeping the two of them apart, even if Winnie wanted to try.

She loved how much Clover adored Amanda. And all the love Amanda showered on her dog. The two of them came together in a scene that belonged in the movies, with Clover whining and yelping with excitement, and Amanda *Cloooover!*-ing back.

Then Amanda fluffed up the fur on Clover's yellow shoulders, and once that ritual was complete, the Labrador went back to grassy rolling.

Winnie just happened to have a baggie full of cookies in the pocket of her purple fleece vest.

Because a short while ago she happened to see a flash of running into Amanda on campus during their morning walk.

"Okay, then, what are you confessing?" Winnie asked her.

"Remember your little robot friend? With the random number generator?"

"Of course. He was my mother."

"Well," Amanda said, starting on her third cookie, "I hid a bunch more of those all around the lab before you all got there. And guess what? These are excellent, by the way." She cleared a smear of jam she could feel on her cheek. "We checked them the next day. And *ta-da*— they weren't so random anymore."

Clover stood up. Shook off her fur. Looked at Winnie and Amanda and happily panted for a second or two. Then, like a gymnast practicing her rolls, she tucked her right shoulder again and aimed it toward the frost-covered grass, dove down, and continued rolling back and forth on her back.

Apparently it never got old.

"Sorry," Winnie told Amanda about her exciting news, "but I don't know what that means."

"It means there was enough energetic cohesiveness in that room that all the robots starting synchronizing their numbers."

"Oh…" Winnie said. "Actually, that does sound interesting."

"It's not normal," Amanda said. "I can tell you that."

She glanced at her watch. Winnie knew any minute Amanda would take the rest of her cookies and run.

"Have you heard from any of the Brits? Or Irina?"

Amanda started jogging in place. The signs were there.

"They sent me a few pictures from Sedona,"

Amanda said. "In one of them you can see through solid rock."

Winnie raised her eyebrows.

"It's a little trick our friend Edgar can do," said Amanda. "I'll tell you more about it later. I need to keep going."

Winnie didn't try to stop her. Neither did Clover, although she did accept a parting gift of more fluffing around her shoulders.

"I actually made those cookies for you," Winnie said. "To thank you. For inviting mc to your party."

"Are you kidding?" Amanda said. "You *made* my party. Not to mention the after-party at your house." Amanda shook her head. "Still can't believe she almost got away without telling us. If not for you…"

Amanda ducked her head in a short bow and saluted two fingers off her cap. Then she started jogging backward. Their time was almost up.

"That was actually a very important experience for me," Winnie said. "I'm really grateful. I just wanted you to know."

Amanda smiled. "I do know. It was important for me, too."

The two of them shared a look, and that was that.

As her friend ran away, at a speed that still amazed Winnie any time she saw it, she thought of the young girl Amanda Birkauer had been.

Sporty already. Lots of friends. Outgoing. Optimistic. Ambitious.

Winnie still felt what it was like to be eight-year-old Amanda, in those brief minutes she and Irina spent inside her head. To feel sad about her parents. Her lack of money. But to always be thinking big, like she still did now.

Clover shook off again. She could do this all day. But Winnie had things to do back at the house.

Arthur was waiting. Winnie had gardening to do. She had invited her niece Rose and husband Matthew and their daughter Annabelle over for dinner the following night. She needed to figure out what to make for them and then shop for ingredients.

But there was one thing more. Winnie had been thinking about it the past few days.

An experiment of her own.

One she would tell Amanda about once it was a little more established. But for now, it was Winnie's and Irina's secret.

A regular date with Irina on Saturday afternoons to practice their telepathy. Winnie had already sent her a message the day before, mentally, and received an immediate and enthusiastic answer. *Yes!*

They would pick a convenient time and then see what they could see. Winnie knew what it felt like to be in the same mind space with Irina. It seemed a shame to let that drop just because they lived in different places.

But there was no distance between telepathic minds. Irina could be on the moon and still send her thoughts to Winnie.

It was a skill Winnie wanted to practice and strengthen for herself.

And there was another reason she wanted to keep in contact with Irina.

The romantic in Winnie didn't want to wait three years to find out the rest of that story. How Irina and Arni met. How they fell in love. Where they lived. What Arni was like.

It was a story Winnie wanted to watch as it unfolded in real time.

Better than any movie. This one was real.

She wasn't sure yet how to hold back her knowledge of Irina's future. Although she still didn't know if Professor Benfry might have already told her.

It was a wide open field. Something Winnie was curious about. And her life now was pursuing the answers to whatever she wanted to know.

That was the mold she was constructing. Made of wonder and discovery. Of exploration and finding out. And cheering on her friends. And sharing their interesting lives. And spending time with her family and with her dogs. And baking. And reading.

Winnie had been thinking about all the pieces of

her new mold. Adding a bit here, and more over there, and watching it take shape little by little.

Here was a spot for telepathy. And here was a spot for Irina. Winnie would keep adding as she went along. She might never be done.

But already she could feel herself pouring into this mold. Feeling out her way to the edges of it. Testing how it fit.

It fit well. It felt good. It felt like it fit her now, for who she was.

"Come on, sweet girl," Winnie called to her dog.

Clover shook herself off one last time and then wagged her tail in a full corkscrew circle. High praise. Winnie would take it.

As she clipped on the leash and aimed them both toward home, Winnie mentally added Clover's examples to her mold:

Take time to play.

Show the people you love how much you love them.

Really love the simple pleasures of life.

Good advice.

Winnie would take it.

NOTE TO READERS

I love to follow the breadcrumbs.

I have read so many wonderful books I never would have known about if I hadn't seen some small, passing reference to them in some other book I was reading.

So allow me to lay some breadcrumbs for you...

Books by Dean Radin, PhD, especially ***The Science of Magic: How the Mind Weaves the Fabric of Reality.***

Books by Frank DeMarco, especially ***The Cosmic Internet*** and ***Rita's World.***

Mind Trek and ***The Ultimate Time Machine*** by Joseph McMoneagle about his experiences with Remote Viewing.

Books by Joseph Gallenberger, PhD, especially ***Inner Vegas: Creating Miracles, Abundance & Health*** and ***Liquid Luck: The Good Fortune Handbook.*** He also teaches courses such as "Inner Vegas Virtual" where you can experiment with psychokinesis and dice throwing. See all his offerings at synccreation.com.

Cheers,

~Robin Brande

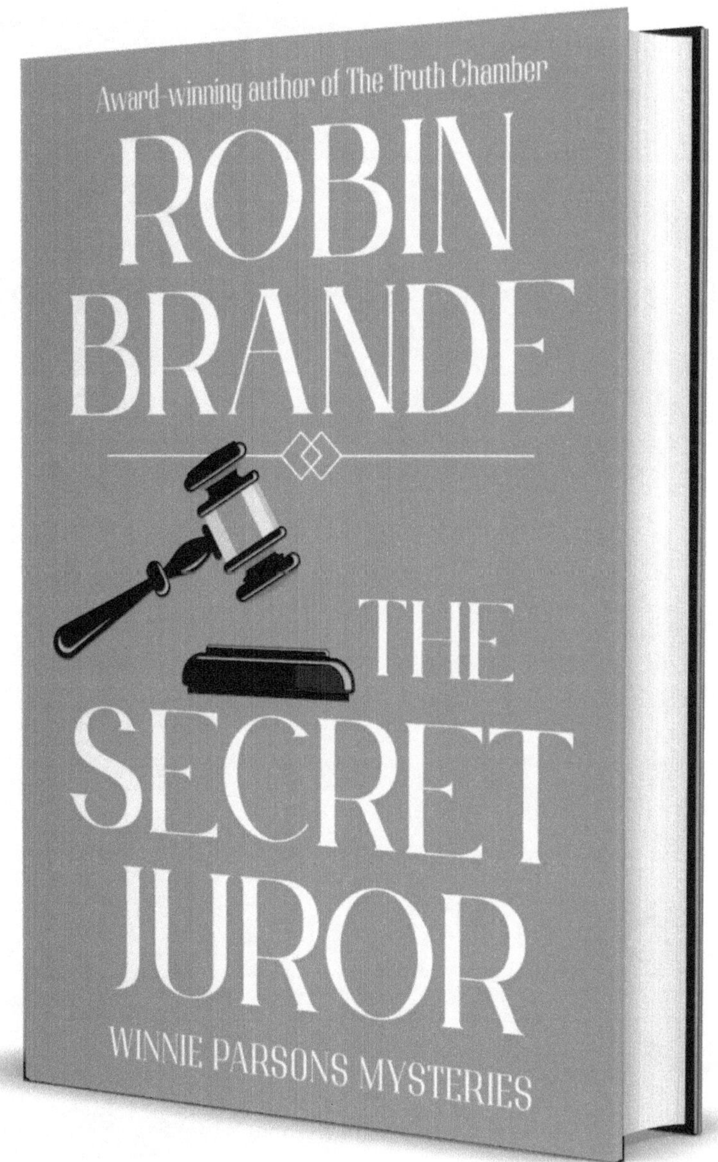

Liars can't hide
from Winnie Parsons.
But they sure keep trying.

5 Winnie Parsons
Mystery Stories

Stories of life after death, miracle healings, communication with other species, and more.

Open up your heart
to the love of a
good dog.

ABOUT THE AUTHOR

Robin Brande is an award-winning author, former trial attorney, black belt in martial arts, wilderness medic, and Reiki Master.

She writes in multiple genres, including mystery, fantasy, science fiction, young adult, romance, and self-help. She is also a designer and maker whose work celebrates the bookish life.

For more information:
robinbrande.com